SCANDALOUS

BY

DENISE HILL

DH Publishing Company
Indianapolis, IN 46229

SCANDALOUS

Cover Design: Kreative Solutions by Mahogani
ISBN:0692571671

Editor: DH Publishing Company

Email address: dhpublishingco@gmail.com
Website: www.dhpublishingco.com

Acknowledgments

Third book!

First and foremost, I want to thank God for allowing me the opportunity to write another book. "God is so good." No one could have told me that I would become a writer. I know I have a wild and crazy imagination, but I never saw myself as someone who would write and publish books. It just goes to show you that God has a plan for your life and it may not be your plan.

I want to thank my son and daughter and my close friends for being supportive and encouraging me to fulfill my dreams and never give up no matter what comes my way. I want to thank my fans who continue to support me. I know you guys are waiting for part 2 of my first and second novel and I promise its coming 2016! Thank you guys so much for being so supportive!

PROLOGUE

Later that night, Trina was sleeping, she was not in a deep sleep when she heard someone out on the balcony jiggling her doorknob. Trina eased out of bed, grabbed her stun gun and inched closer to the door. She stood there for a minute and then swiftly opened it.

"What the hell are you doing here?" She said as she startled him.

"Oh shit! You scared the daylights out of me," Martin said as he leaned in and tried to kiss Trina, but she backed away.

"Now don't be like that babe."

"How dare you come to me after you slept with Gloria this morning? You got me twisted if you think I'm going to fuck you after that. Go to her damn room and stay out of mine and by the way, I'm leaving tomorrow heading back home and if I hear of you being here with Gloria, I will turn your ass in so fast. Do I make myself clear?"

"You should be mad at your friend as well. She's the one that's been contacting me to come and fuck her. Does she know anything about us?"

"Why the fuck would she?"

"I just figured she was trying to make you jealous."

"Jealous, jealous of what?"

"Oh, it's like that now."

"What are you talking about?"

"Are you saying I'm nothing?"

"Boy, I don't have time for this."

"Boy, I got your boy right here and when you want it, let me know and don't make me wait too long. You know, you are really tripping because I definitely ain't no damn boy." Martin pulled his dick out. "What boy has a dick like this and can make plenty of women fall in love with it. Huh, you tell me."

Scandalous

CHAPTER ONE

"**Tracy,** I don't understand it. I go out every weekend and I still can't meet the right person?" Judy said as she stood in Tracy's bathroom applying her mascara to her eyelashes.

Tracy looked at Judy sideways.

"The right person, who's the right person?" Tracy asked.

"You know the tall, dark handsome man with a good heart that will love me forever and take care of me so I can't stop working this 9 to 5."

"Girl boo! You better settle for what you can get and call it a day. Not everyone can meet someone like that. You have to be a very special person and let's just say you're not that special."

"What? I beg your pardon."

"Beg my pardon, nothing. You know you're this close to looking like Precious," Tracy said as she snapped her finger.

"Now a person like me, I can attract men like that just watch and see who I pull tonight."

Judy rolled her eyes at Tracy she was hotter than a fat man in hell at her for saying she was this close to looking like precious.

"Hell precious will never look this damn good, old funky bitch," Judy said under her breath.

Judy and Tracy had only been friends for about four months. They met at work when Tracy was promoted as the Executive Secretary to the President of the company. From day one, the women connected and had been friends since, but Judy had been a little envious of Tracy on the down low. Tracy seemed to have it all from the nice job to the nice apartment and not to mention she got all the male attention, but little did Judy know Tracy doesn't have her act together as much as she wanted others to think. She's robbing Peter to pay Paul, she's three months behind on her car note and as far as men, she cannot keep a man around. Oh, she can get their attention, but keeping them is another thing.

"So where are we going tonight, Miss Lady?" Judy asked.

"We are going to a nice club where wealthy men hang out." She said as she walked pass Judy winking her eye. Judy got excited just the thought of meeting someone that could possibly take care of her. Judy was longing for that Knight in shining armor. She wanted someone to sweep her off her feet and take care of her forever.
Judy followed Tracy to her bedroom and stood at the door.

"What shoes should I wear?" Tracy asked as she held up two expensive pairs of shoes.

"I think the black Christian Louboutin look better with that outfit."

"Then Louboutin it is. These shoes here were a present from one of my wealthy friends. You see I only date men with money. I have no time for broke ass men wanting me to take care of them. That's the problem with these women today they settle too much. I refuse to settle for anything less than what I deserve."

"So why did you tell me to settle?"

"Because people like you have to settle. You will never be able to get what I get so settling is the best thing for people like you."

"What do you mean people like me?"

"Well, you know people who are not that attractive and a little overweight."

"I can't believe you just said that. I can't believe you are that stupid to think that."

"Stupid! Girl please, you and I both know this is true. Can you name one person who is unattractive, overweight and is married or dating a wealthy good looking man?" Tracy stood and waited for Judy to answer.

"See, you can't think of one person can you? You might think I'm being hurtful, but believe me, I am only being honest."
Now, Tracy had Judy feeling bad about herself. Judy glanced at herself in the mirror. "Maybe she's right. I could stand to lose at least 30 pounds and invest in some better

makeup." She said as she turned sideways to see just how big she really looked.

Thirty minutes later, the two women exited Tracy's apartment and walked down the walkway to the awaiting cab.

"I don't understand why we are taking a cab and not your car?"

"Girl I don't drink and drive and anyway if I meet someone, what if he wants me to go home with him I don't want to worry about driving my car."

"Oh, okay," Judy said with a confused look on her face. Little did Judy know Tracy was hiding her car from the repo man. She was determined to keep her car hidden until she found a sugar daddy to help her get caught up on her payments. She had Judy believing that she took the bus to work because it was more convenient for her and less expensive to park which was true, but that was not the reason she took the bus every day.

As the women made their way through the crowded club to a booth over in the corner of the room, Martin was sitting at the bar when he spotted an attractive woman who put him in the mind of Gabrielle Union. Martin checked her out from head to toe. He noticed how she was scanning the room he only hoped she was not looking for her man.
Martin continued to watch as the two women took their seats. He quickly flagged over a waitress and sent her over to their table to buy them both a drink.
The waitress made her way over to Tracy and Judy.

"What would you ladies like to drink tonight and just to let you know, the handsome man across the room is paying for your drink."

"Are you serious?" Judy asked.

"Yes, he said he's paying so if there's anything you ladies want, it's on him."

"Why don't you tell him to come over and join us?" Tracy said.

Tracy watched as a tall, handsome, well-built man walked toward their table. She hoped this was the man buying their drink for them, but as she continued to watch, she saw his gaze was in another direction. She was so busy focusing on the man that she never saw Martin Jackson as he approached their table. Judy sat there with her mouth wide opened as she gazed up at the strikingly handsome man who stood before them. He looked like a model that just left the runway. The gray suit against his dark skin looked good, especially with the pink shirt. Judy looked down at his shoes the gray shoes were the same color gray as his eyes, this man looked like a million dollars she couldn't believe he was standing at their table. Judy kicked Tracy underneath the table to get her attention.

"Oh, my," Tracy said, thinking out loud as she made eye contact with Martin. The chemistry between the two was so powerful that Martin felt a pulling in his groin area. This was something that had never happened to him when meeting someone for the first time, but Tracy felt it too. Looking into his eyes was so mesmerizing.

Martin chuckled after seeing the effect he had on Tracy.

"Hi, I'm Martin Jackson." He said as he held out his hand.

"Hi, I'm Tracy and this is my friend Judy. It was really nice of you to buy us a drink tonight." Tracy said as Martin held her hand.

"It's the least I can do for such beautiful women."

The women smiled from ear to ear. Judy scooted over as if Martin wanted to sit next to her, but instead, he slid in right next to Tracy.

"Another one for her," Judy uttered under her breath. This was why Judy secretly envied Tracy. Judy was looking for someone with a good heart while Tracy only cared about how much a person was worth, fuck a good heart Tracy would always say. How can a good heart pay my bills or buy me the latest fashions?

Judy was so tired of women like Tracy getting all the wealthy men and leaving the bums for the real women. Tracy and Martin sat talking for hours, they talked so much that they bored the hell out of Judy so she decided to leave.

"Well, you guys, it's been real, but I think I'm going to call it a night. It was nice meeting you Martin. Tracy, I'll see you tomorrow and don't do anything I wouldn't do." She said as she got up to leave.

"Be careful," Tracy said.

Tracy and Martin continue to talk when he heard his favorite song from Wale featuring Usher called Matrimony.

"Would you like to dance?"

"Sure, why not."

On the dance floor, Tracy laid her head against Martin's chest as she took in the smell of his cologne and the hardness of his chest. She noticed the feel of his powerful hands as they lay against her back. Tracy glanced up and noticed Martin's lips. She would do anything to feel his lips against hers. Martin caught Tracy staring at him and smiled.

"Is everything okay?' He said as he bent down and whispered in her ear.

"Yes, I'm fine. I was just admiring you."

"Oh, I'm glad you like what you see?"

"Definitely," Tracy said as she looked up at him and smiled.

Martin bent down and brushed his lips against hers. The feel of his lips and the smell of his cologne drove her crazy. Tracy slowly opened her mouth to allow Martin's tongue to enter. The smell of him and the way he kissed her made her pussy throb. She felt him against her stomach, then all of a sudden he broke away from her.

"Damn baby you have no idea what you are doing to me."

"You know I could say the same about you."

"Oh really, can we continue this back at my place."

"Why don't we continue this tomorrow? It's getting pretty late and I'm afraid I wouldn't be good company tonight." Tracy didn't want Martin to think she was easy so she decided to make him wait for the cookies.

"Whatever you say."
Martin escorted Tracy back to the booth where she grabbed her coat.

"Oh, I almost forgot, I'm not driving so is there any way you can give me a ride home?"

"No problem sweetheart."
Martin helped Tracy put her coat on before they exited the club. Tracy was so interested in seeing what type of car Martin drove. Standing outside waiting on the valet person all types of cars ran through her head when a silver Bentley pulled up. Tracy continued to look on when she noticed the valet person handing Martin the keys to the Bentley.

"You have got to be kidding me." Tracy said."

"What are you talking about?"

"Is this what you're driving?"

"Yes, is there something wrong with it?"

"No, not at all. I'm just surprised."
Martin laughed.

"Sweetheart, just wait until you get to know me. On the ride home, Tracy imagined how Martin's home looked. If his home looked anything like his car, she knew she had hit the jackpot. Martin stood at least 6'2 medium size build. His complexion was dark brown with gray eyes. His hair was cut low and he sported a nicely trimmed goatee. He was sexy as hell and had a calm demeanor about himself. He could have any woman he chose, this was what frightened Tracy.
Tracy had never been insecure about anything until now. "Am I good enough for him?" She thought to herself. "Calm down Tracy don't get ahead of yourself." She thought to herself.
Martin looked over at Tracy. "Are you okay over there?"

"Yes, I'm just tired. I think the alcohol has gotten the best of me." Tracy lied.
Martin pulled up to Tracy's apartment building. He exited the car, walked around to the passenger side and opened the door for Tracy. The two walked silently hand in hand to her

front door. Martin touched the side of her face with his hand.

"Can I see you tomorrow?"

"Sure."

Martin leaned in and kissed Tracy softly on the lips. Tracy pulled him in a little closer and went in for the kill. She loved the feel of his soft lips against hers and having his body close to her was all she needed. There was something about Martin that drove her crazy and made her a little uneasy.

Tracy pulled away while she could and said good night to Martin.

"Good night sweetheart," Martin said as he walked away. Tracy stood in the doorway watching his sexy ass body as he walked to his car.

"Damn that man is going to drive me fucking crazy. I can already tell," She said as she shut her front door.

CHAPTER TWO

The ringing of the phone jarred Tracy out of her sleep. She looked at the clock on the nightstand before answering.

"Hello".

"Don't tell me you are still in bed."

"Yes, I am. I have to admit I stayed out later than I had planned."

"What time are you planning on gracing us with your presence?"

"Didn't I tell you I was off today and Monday?"

"No, you didn't. What are you doing this evening?"

"Martin and I are going to dinner this evening and we'll probably catch a movie or something. Why?"

"Um… so you're going out with him already?" Judy asked with jealousy in her voice.

"Do I detect a little jealousy?"

"Girl, please! I'm just used to us hanging out on Friday's that's all. So do you like this guy?"

"Yes, so far, so good. He seems nice and seems to have his shit together. Actually, he seems too good to be true."

"I hope you're right."

"Alright Judy let me get off this phone so I can go back to sleep and I will call you a little later."

Later that day, Tracy was busy cleaning her apartment and getting things ready for her date tonight and had forgotten to call Judy so Judy decided to call her. She already had an attitude because Tracy was the one who was chosen last night.

"Hello."

"Oh, I see how you are now. Since you met someone last night you can't call your friend now?"

"Judy what are you talking about. I have been cleaning my apartment all day and trying to find something to wear for my date. I had planned to call you before I took my bath. What crawled up your ass today?"

"Nothing, I will call you later since you're too busy for me now."

Before Tracy could say anything, Judy had hung up the phone.

"You bitch," Tracy yelled as she dropped the phone on the bed.

Martin decided to prepare dinner for Tracy at his place. Not often does he feel this comfortable bringing someone here, but with Tracy, he felt as though she was his soul mate.

"So where are you taking me?"

"I decided to bring you to my home for dinner and show you some of my hospitality. I had my chef prepare dinner and dessert for us."

"A chef I didn't know you had it like that."

Martin laughed.

"You will learn everything about me in due time and in return, I want to know all there is to know about Tracy Simmons," He said as he patted Tracy on her knee.

"Here's a little information about me." He said as he turned the corner heading for the interstate.

"My family owned an investment firm that was passed down to me and my brother when my parents passed away. My brother and I are worth 5.5 million, so you see, money is not an issue for me. If things work out as I hope they do, you will get to enjoy the fruit from my tree."

Tracy almost had a heart attack, she could not believe what she was hearing. She felt like asking Martin to pull over so she could get out of the car and turn some flips.

"Oh my God, just wait until I tell Judy," she said to herself.

As Martin continued to tell Tracy about him, all she could see was dollar signs and that she had hit the jackpot.

As the car approached what looked like a mansion, Tracy had to pinch herself to make sure she was not dreaming. She had never seen anything like it. Martin's home was huge and to think, this could be her home at some point. Martin got out, walked around to the passenger side and opened the door for Tracy.

"You're such a gentleman."

"Always for you, sweetheart."

Martin escorted her in the house through the garage. "OMG, I can't believe how big this kitchen is. It is bigger than my entire apartment."

"I had this kitchen remodeled last year to enlarge it. Come on let me give you a full tour while the chef prepares dinner."

Martin gave Tracy a tour of the home and she fell in love.

"Oh God, I cannot believe someone lives in a home like this. This is the type of home you see on television."

"I take it you have never been in a home like this before."

"No, I have only seen homes like this in the movies."

After the tour, Martin took her to the dining area where his chef awaited their arrival.

"Tracy this is Calvin, my chef."

"Nice to meet you, Tracy."

Martin pulled out her chair and waited until she was comfortably seated before he walked around the table to take his seat.

"I hope you enjoy your meal," Calvin said before walking away shaking his head.

Later that evening after dinner, Martin and Tracy sat by the fireplace having drinks.

"I still can believe how beautiful your home is. How long have you lived here."

"This was actually my parents' home and when they passed away, I inherited the house. I have lived here for almost two years now.

"Why?"

"I can't believe you live here alone. Why aren't you married?"

"Why aren't you married?" Martin asked her.

"Oh, I see you're going to answer a question with a question."

Martin chuckled.

"You are something else I see. I think I could get used to you hanging around. How about you, could you get used to being around me?"

"Not sure just yet, ask me again in a couple of months," Tracy said as she hid a smile from Martin. Then she burst out laughing.

"I'm just kidding, I definitely could get used to hanging out with you.

"Come here." He said as he took her drink and sat it down on the coffee table. He pulled her onto his lap and buried his tongue deep inside her mouth as he allowed a moan to escape.

"I don't know what you are doing to me lady, but I'm loving it," He said as he started to unbutton her blouse and slowly laid her down on the carpet where he pulled one of her breasts free and ran his tongue across the nipple causing her to moan.

"Oh, Martin baby please that turns me on."

"I am going to do more than turn you on." Martin said as he began to pull her skirt down and then her panties. He planted his head between her thighs and stuck his tongue inside her, as he tasted her juices. He then ran his tongue across her clit, causing her to shudder. She pulled his head closer as both hands lay on the back of his head, pulling him in closer and closer until he could barely breathe.

"Oh, Martin this feels so damn good baby. I want you inside me now." Tracy yelled.

"Your wish is my command."

Martin stood and unbuttoned his belt and removed his pants. He pulled his boxers down, unwrapped the condom and placed it on his penis. He bent down, crawled between Tracy's legs and inserted himself slowly inside her wetness.

"Oh shit," Martin said as he began to move slowly in and out of her pussy. Baby girl you're going to make me fall madly in love with you if I'm not careful."

"Martin please, harder baby it feels so damn good. Ooh, Martin baby, I'm about to come."
Martin began to move in deeper and deeper, faster and faster until he exploded a couple of seconds after she did.

"Oh shit, that was a good one babe."

The two lay silently on the carpet in front of the fireplace until Tracy remembered Calvin. "Where is Calvin? Is he still here?"

"Why are you worried about Calvin?"

"I just hope he wasn't here while we were having sex."

"Oh, don't worry, he's not here."

"I guess I should get you home."

"What, oh, I see fuckem and then take them home."

"Naw, it's nothing like that. You are welcome to stay sweetheart if you want to."

"It's okay, you can take me home."

"Are you sure you don't want to stay?"

"I'm sure. There will be other times for me to stay."

"I hope so," Martin said as he brushed his lips across Tracy's lips.

On the ride home, Tracy was a little confused at Martin's eagerness to get rid of her at the mention of Calvin's name.

"What's up with that she said to herself?"

As soon as Tracy made it home, she pulled her phone out to call Judy. As soon as she mentioned Martin's name, Tracy could sense Judy's resentment.

"Girl, what is up with you and that attitude? I just called to tell you about my date with Martin and to tell you about his mansion.
Judy stood holding the phone to her ear, pretending to be interested in what Tracy had to say.

"Tracy all I can say is just be careful. Everything that glitters isn't gold. When are we going to hang out..., tomorrow?"

"No Martin and I have plans, sorry Judy and don't go thinking that I am putting Martin before you because I'm not."

"Yeah, whatever, action speaks a lot louder than words. You have already canceled out on me today for Martin and now tomorrow."

"Judy don't be like that if it were you I would be so happy for you."

"It's not that I not happy for you, it's just something about him that doesn't sit well with me."

"Judy you don't even know him. You met him once, and now you say there's something about him that you don't like. Judy come on don't be like that you are my girl and I want you to be happy for me."

"I told you I was happy for you. Look, Tracy, I'm getting ready to go to bed, I will talk with you later."
Judy didn't even wait for Tracy to respond she just hung the phone up and hopped into bed.

"I can't believe she had the nerve to call me and rub it in my face about her Mr. Right. Hell, I hope he turns out to be Mr. So Fucking Wrong," Judy said as she made herself comfortable in bed.

As the days and weeks went by, Judy and Tracy spent less and less time with each other and that was fine with Judy because it began to make her sick to hear Tracy constantly brag about Martin. It was always Martin this and Martin that.

CHAPTER THREE

Tracy and Martin continued to see each other on a regular basis. She would spend two or three nights a week with him. He started hinting about her moving in with him, but she was still not sure about him. He would even drop off roses to her at work or stop by the office just to take her to lunch. This irked the hell out of Judy.

Tracy would even invite Judy to tag along with them to lunch, but she was such a Debbie downer that Tracy just stopped inviting her.

One day Tracy was busy working when Judy and a co-worker appeared at her desk. Tracy looked up and saw Judy standing there smiling from ear to ear. "Hey, Judy, what's up?"

"Girl this is my new friend Carol and girl she has got some news for you about Martin."

"What do you mean?"

"I'll let her tell you."

"So you're the one dating that fine ass Martin Jackson?" Tracy gave Carol an evil eye.

"Yeah, and what's it to you?"

"Oh, don't go getting your panties in a knot. I am only here to warn you. Martin is not the man you think he is, just be careful."

"What are you talking about?"

"Why don't you ask him?"

"No, I'm asking you. You bring some bullshit to me at work about him not being who I think he is. You tell me?"

"I used to date Martin.

Tracy looked Carol up and down and by the way she looked with her big fat ass she could tell that Martin would never date anyone that looked like that.

"Girl please stop wasting my fucking time."

"Oh, so you think I'm lying since I am overweight and not as attractive as you are? Is that what it is? Martin has a big thick dick doesn't he and right above it is a tattoo, right? I used to fuck with him a couple of years ago. He's a charmer and can charm the panties off any woman. I found that out when I caught him in bed with my roommate." Tracy looked back at Judy, who was still smiling."

"What the fuck are you so happy about?" Tracy asked Judy.

"Don't get mad at me because your Mr. Right ain't really right."

"Sorry to bust your fucking bubble, but your friend has not said anything that makes me believe he's not Mr. Right. She just said she dated him a couple of years ago and he fucked her roommate. Well, if I looked like you Carol, I don't blame Martin for cheating on you." Tracy laughed as she turned back around to finish doing her work and then thought about what Judy was trying to do and turn back around to face Judy and Carol.

"You know what Judy and Carol. You guys ain't nothing but haters and haters, I don't do so kick rocks you big bitches."

The next day when Tracy arrived at work, she walked in on Judy, Carol, and some other women talking about her. As she walked further into the break room, she cleared her throat to let them know she was there and well aware of their conversation about her.

"I guess you sorry bitches have nothing better to do but to meddle all up in my business. Well, here's a bit of information for you. Martin asked me to move in with him last night. I will let you know if I decide to do that so you will have something to talk about since it's clear that neither one of you have any business of your own. Good day ladies."

Tracy walked away laughing, leaving them looking stupid as hell.

Tracy walked back to her desk in tears. She was hurt she never thought Judy would have turned on her like that. It took every bone in her body not to cry right in front of the other women so she played it off by laughing.

Tracy retrieved her phone from her purse and made her way to the bathroom. When she entered, she checked all the stalls just to make sure she was alone. Tracy dialed Martin, who answered on the first ring and soon as she heard his voice, she started balling.

"Hey, hey, what's wrong?" Martin asked.

"Martin I can't believe Judy would turn on me like this."

"Oh, babe I told you she's just jealous. Don't let her or anyone else get you upset like this. Man, you need to leave early and come home and be with me."

"I wish I could, but I can't, I have too much work to do and I have a deadline to meet. I'm sorry I called you with this mess. I just needed to hear your voice."

"Don't be sorry. I am glad you called because I was just sitting here thinking about you. I really wish you would consider moving in here with me because I get lonely when you're not here."

"Aw, you're so sweet. I am starting to miss you when you're not around, especially at night when I'm at my place.

"See all the more reasons why you should move in with me."

"Baby I will really think about it, okay. Let me get off this phone and get back to work. I'll call you a little later."

Tracy had a meeting with her boss and was on her way back to her desk when Judy stopped her.

"Tracy I am so sorry that our friendship went south because I really do care about your well-being. I in no way wanted to hurt you like you had hurt me, I just wanted you to know what type of person you're dealing with."

"What do you mean how I've hurt you?"

"Tracy, you have no idea how your words have hurt me when you told me that I was close to looking like Precious and that I had to settle for whatever I could get. That hurt me to the core and you thought nothing of it."

"Judy I never meant to hurt your feelings I was just being honest so I thought. I guess I could have said it in a better way. I am so sorry that I hurt you Judy, but that doesn't mean you had to hurt me back. You should have told me that I hurt your feelings. An eye for an eye… huh, that's not like you. You know I've been thinking and I think it's best that we give our friendship a break for a while." Tracy said as she made her way back to her desk.

Judy felt some kind of way about Tracy's comment, but she finally agreed that it was for the best that they give their friendship a break. It was not like her to hurt someone because they hurt her, maybe Carol was rubbing off on her she thought.

Later that evening Tracy and Martin were out having dinner when out of nowhere Carol appeared.

"Hello, Martin Jackson."

"Hello, Carol how are you?"

"I was telling Tracy earlier today about us dating a couple of years ago. I guess she didn't believe me because I'm so chunky."

Martin choked on his water when Carol said this.

"Did she ask you about us?"

"I sorry Carol but no she didn't."

"I didn't ask him Carol because it doesn't really matter. I have dated other people in the past as well, so I don't see what the big fucking deal is. So he dated a butterball. I'm pretty sure there are plenty of men out here who have or is currently dating a lard ass."

Martin was shocked hearing this coming from Tracy, but he understood why. Carol was trying to make a mountain out of a Moe hill she was trying to tear their relationship apart and Tracy wasn't having it. I hope that this will be the end to Carol's scheme.

Several weeks later, Tracy and Martin boarded the plan that would take them to his beach house in Los Angeles on Hermosa Beach. Tracy was excited, to say the least as the plane took off. This was her first time flying and she's doing it with the man she loved.

"I can't wait to see the beach and to see your beach house. I feel like I'm dreaming and have been since I met you."

"Well, sweetheart, you're not dreaming this is real, all too real." Martin smiled nervously.

Six hours later, they pulled in the back of the beach home. Still anxious, Tracy could not wait to see the beach. Martin pulled into the garage and decided to give her a view of the beach before going inside.

"Come, my dear, the beach is awaiting you," Martin said as he grabbed her hand and walked her in the direction of the beach.

"Oh, this is awesome," Tracy said smiling.

"I'm glad you like it," It gave Martin great pleasure seeing Tracy so happy.

Martin showed her the boardwalk where the bikers and skaters came out every day. He took her to the outdoor restaurants and of course, he showed her some clothing stores before heading to his beach home.

When they entered the beach house, her mouth flew open. She was amazed and especially as she walked further into the home and up the stairs where she saw the living room view. It was the view of the Pacific Ocean.

"OMG Martin this is fabulous. I would love to live here all year round. Can we please?"

"Oh, now you want to live with me." Martin laughed. "You are too much Tracy Simmons."

Tracy laughed as she playfully hit Martin in the arm.

"I would never leave this room."

"The bedroom on the next floor has the same view and it has a balcony."

"Oh well, I would never leave that room."

"Are you hungry?" Martin asked.

"Yes, can we go to the restaurant that we passed that played the light jazz that faces the ocean?"

"Let me take our luggage to the bedroom and then we can head out."

Tracy felt as though she was on top of the world. She just hoped and prayed that things never changed between her and Martin and if they did change, she hoped it would be for the better, but she believed this couldn't get any better.

"This is heaven," Tracy said as she fed her face, listened to some light jazz, and sipped on a Corona as the view of the Pacific Ocean greeted her.

"I would be willing to quit my job and give up my apartment to live here forever."

"Is that so?"

"Can we walk along the boardwalk after we finish here?"

"We can do whatever you want, sweetheart. This trip is for you. You deserved to get away from the madness at the workplace so just enjoy yourself."

"Martin you're too good to me. What did I do to deserve someone like you?"

"I don't know, seeing how you talked to Carol the way you did the other day…. Hum."

"Oh, so you think I was wrong for saying what I said. Do you know what she told me? She had the nerve to tell me how big your private part was and that you slept with her roommate while you were dating her and that you are not the person I think you are."

"What!"

"Don't believe any of that bullshit she's talking about. I took her out a couple of times and I didn't even have sex with her. I said I had a tattoo and that's when she tried to pull my pants down so she could see and she felt my Jimmie. And as far as me sleeping with Daisy her roommate, yeah I did. She wanted it and so I gave it to her. Big mistake, that girl stalked me for months."

"Dang, you put it on her like that?"

"Well, you know how I do it."

"Whatever. Tracy said as she pushed Martin.

"You know I'm not lying. When I put it down, I put it down. I got you hooked."

Tracy rolled her eyes.

29

"You make me sick."

"No, I make you feel good, real good," Martin said as he grabbed a hold of Tracy by her waist and pulled her against him. "You feel that? That's what you do to me. Just looking at you gets me aroused."

"Martin baby don't do this to me right now. I'm trying to enjoy the scenery and you're going to make me take that ass back to the house."

"And what are you going to do to me at the house." Martin said as he nibbled on her ear before running his tongue inside."

"Martin please stop! You know damn well that makes me weak."

"Okay, I'll stop, but just until we get back to the house and then it's on."

"Bet," Tracy said as she hooked her arm around Martin's waist as they walked along the boardwalk.
Tracy enjoyed the view of the other beach homes along the Pacific Ocean. The feeling that came over her as she walked with Martin was intoxicating.

"Martin babe I love you so much. I want to spend the rest of my life with you right here."

"Aw, babe I love you as well. Would you really give up everything to move out here?"

"At this moment I would say yes, but it would be something I would seriously consider once we get back home. I think we should sit down and talk about it."

"We can do that. You know my heart is where ever you are."

"That's so sweet. You say the sweetest things. Did you say things like this to Carol?" Tracy laughed.

"You're so funny."

That night the two lay in bed with the balcony doors open as the wind from the ocean blew in. The sound of the waves amazed Tracy.

"This is too cool." She said as she eased out of bed to stand in the entryway of the balcony.

Martin eased up behind her and removed her nightshirt. He moved his hand across her breast as his other hand moved to her waist and bent her over. He began to run his penis up and down the front of her pussy to the back of her ass before inserting it into her vagina. Then he stroked her slow and easy in and out as the juices' from her pussy made slurping sounds. His strokes became harder and deeper.

"Oh, baby this feels so good. Tracy said as she clamped her pussy wall tight around his penis.

"That's it baby squeeze the hell out of this dick take it all."

"Oh, oh, oh baby, I'm coming. Come with me." Martin yelled.

"I'm coming baby."

"Aw, that was so damn good," Martin said as he continued to slowly stroke her.

"Aw baby, I'm coming again," Tracy said as she grinds harder against his dick. "Oh Martin please I need it, give it all to me."

Legs wobbly Martin gave it all to Tracy.

"Damn, what are you trying to do to me woman."

"You're the one that's got me all horny and shit with that big thick dick of yours."

"Well, you know what can I say." Martin chuckled. Once they finally made it to the bed, Martin and Tracy lay awake talking about their future together.

"Do you want kids Martin?"

"Yes, I want tons of kids."

"Tons how many is tons?"

Martin was tickled.

"I'm just messing with you. I want at least two boys and a girl. How about you?"

"I'll give you two, but that's it."

"Why not three?"

"I don't know. I would have to really think hard about that."

"That's cool."

"Would you allow your wife to work?"

"I would, but only after the kids are in school."

"Would it bother you if I asked you to quit working?"

"It depends on...."

"It depends on what? If I ask you to quit it means I would take care of you. Anything you wanted and needed I would provide for you."

"Oh well if it's like that then hell yeah I would quit." Tracy moved closer to Martin and laid her head on his chest and listen to the ocean as she fell into a deep sleep. Martin laid there for another hour or so before he fell asleep. Martin was so in love with Tracy he wanted to give her the world because she deserved it, but his only problem was how he would be able to do that because losing her was not an option.

The next few days flew by quickly. Martin took Tracy into town to do some shopping. They went to the mall and down to Santé Alley where she lost her mind. Martin allowed Tracy to shop as long as she wanted and she enjoyed the freedom to be able to buy whatever she wanted when she wanted. Tracy was surprised when Martin handed her a credit card with her name on it. He gave her a limit of three thousand a day. They shopped so much that they had to buy more luggage in order to carry back the new items they had purchased. This had been the best trip that Tracy had ever had. Tracy thought about Judy, she would love to bring Judy here to shop once their friendship was back to where it used to be.

"I can't believe we are back home already. I am feeling so depressed right now. Honey, can we move to Hermosa Beach now and forget Indiana for good?"

"It will take some time for us to be able to do this you know I have a business to run here."

"I know, but can't your brother run the business?"

"He could if he was here. See, he's out of the country for a while."

"Oh well, at least I tried."

"Come with me on the deck." Martin guided Tracy to the deck in the back to have a talk with her.

"Have you thought any more about what I asked you about moving in with me?"

"Yes I have and I decided to move in with you within a week or so. You know I will be breaking my lease."

"Let me know what you'll own them and I will give you a check to cover it."

"Thanks, babe." Tracy said as she leaned over and gave Martin a kiss on the lips."

"Let me know when you plan to move so I can have the movers move your stuff into a storage unit that I have."

CHAPTER FOUR

Two months later, Martin asked Tracy to quit her job and she did. He supplied her with a weekly allowance and for her birthday, Martin gave her a white Mercedes and hired a driver for her. Tracy thought she had died and gone to heaven. Unfortunately, not everyone was happy for her. Judy stopped speaking to her when she quit her job and moved in with Martin. She despised Tracy because she believed Tracy was a fake person who continued to get things that she felt she deserved because she was a good person inside and out and Tracy was nothing more than a gold digger. Judy had a hard time dealing with the fact that Tracy landed a millionaire and she had no one.

After moving in with Martin, things seemed so great with the two. Martin would take her on day trips, they would take trips to the spa and Martin would close the spa down so it would be just the two of them, but he no longer talked about moving to LA, and that was okay just as long as they could go back to vacation there. Tracy couldn't ask for a better person, but weeks later she noticed how paranoid and secretive Martin had become. She continued to question his behavior to the point where he got agitated and they would argue about it nonstop. Tracy secretly regretted giving up her apartment and her job.

Early one morning, Martin eased out of bed. He looked back at Tracy, who was still sleeping. He loved this woman so much and he felt bad for what he was about to do. Martin slipped on his pants, shirt, and shoes and walked over to the closet where he pulled out two big suitcases and walked to the door, he turned around to take one more look at Tracy before leaving.

A couple hours later, Tracy awakened to find a couple standing over her in bed.

"Oh shit," Tracy yelled.

"What the hell are you doing in our bed?" The woman asked.

Tracy pulled the covers up to her neck and looked over at Martin, but he was not there.

"What are you talking about?" Tracy asked.

"Ron honey, go call the police."

"Wait, the police there has to be some misunderstanding. This is my boyfriend's home." Tracy said as she rose up to a sitting position.

"And who might that be?"

"Martin Jackson."

"Oh my God," the woman said as she grabbed her forehead. And who are you?"

"I'm Tracy Simmons and you are?"

"I'm Trina Patterson and this is my husband Ron."

"Oh well, I moved in here with Martin after he convinced me to quit my job and give up my apartment. I've been living here with him for about two months now." Tracy said as she tried to call Martin on his cell phone to find out that it had been disconnected. Then she called him at work to learn that Martin Jackson was not an employee there.

"Come on Sarah I met you last week when Martin and I stopped by his office."

"Yes, I remember, but still Martin Jackson is not an employee here. He comes by twice a week to water the plants for Mr. Patterson whenever they leave the country. Tracy hung up from talking with Sarah.

"This can't be happening to me. I just tried calling him and his phone is disconnected. Then I called his job and they told me that there's no Martin Jackson employed there, but I was just there last week with him and had a conversation with his secretary. Now she tells me that Martin comes in twice a week to water the plants and that's it. This is just too strange."

The woman walked over and took a seat on the loveseat by the window.

"Honey Martin Jackson was our gardener. We fired him six months ago right before we left the country for sleeping with our housekeeper in our bed and stealing money from us."

"What."

"Where did Martin tell you he worked?" Ron asked.

"He told me that he and his brother inherited JP Investments when their parents passed away."

"JP Investments is me and my brother's company," Ron said.

"I'm sorry sweetheart that you are involved in Martin's latest scheme. You're not the first and you probably won't be the last until he is behind bars where he belongs. We also found out that he had been using our Beach home in Hermosa pretending that he lives there bringing all types of women there. He had to have made copies of all our keys. We need to have all the locks changed ASAP."

"Oh my God, what am I going to do? I quit my job, gave up my apartment and my car when Martin gave me a car for my birthday. He gave me a white Mercedes after I turned my car in for my birthday. Whose car is that?"

"I'm afraid to say that is probably my pearly white Mercedes."

"What about Calvin? He was here and prepared dinner for us."

"I fired Calvin as our cook the same week I fired Martin. They are both schemers so I fired them both for doing the same thing."

Tracy ran her hand over her face.

"I can't believe this. I knew he was too good to be true. I am so sorry about all of this. I guess I'll get my belongings and leave. I don't know where I will go, but I know I have to get out of here." Tracy said as she eased out of bed.

"We'll wait for you downstairs the couple said.

Downstairs in the family room, the couple discussed the situation about Tracy.

"Ron we can't let her leave like this. She has nowhere to go."

"Trina honey this is none of our concern. Our concern is Martin Jackson and why he continues to use our things pretending to be us."

"I know, but Ron I feel responsible for this. If I had let you press charges against Martin when you wanted to, none of this would have happened."

"Well, all right sweetheart, whatever you want to do."

"That's why I love you so much," Trina said as she pinched her husband's cheek.

As Tracy made her way downstairs, Trina greeted her.

"After speaking with my husband, we both agreed to allow you to stay in one of our guest rooms until you find employment and your own place. I kind of feel responsible for Martin's scheme."

"Oh my God, are you guys sure?"

"Yes, we are."

"Thank you so much I really appreciate this," Tracy said as she followed behind Trina who showed her the guest room.

"I don't know how I am going to repay you guys for your kindness, but I will think of some way."

"Oh, don't be silly. You don't owe us anything."

"Yes, I do. You don't know me and you are willing to allow me to live in your home. I would say I owe you my life seeing that I have nothing not even a dime to my name. By the way, here is a credit card Martin gave me to use I guess this probably belongs to you." Tracy said as she handed Trina the credit card.

"Um… this is probably tied to Ron's account. I'll have this canceled and I won't tell them why so this will keep you out of trouble."

"Thank you. When I can, I will repay for all the purchases I made using the card. It may take me some time, but I will pay you I promise."

"Don't worry about it and make yourself at home. I will have Louise make us some breakfast and I'll come and get you when breakfast is ready." Trina said as she exited the room.

Tracy looked around the room and was grateful that the Patterson's were so understanding of her situation if they hadn't she would definitely be out on the street. She still can't believe what had happened. She can't believe Martin was such a fraud. How can anyone be so cruel she thought? "I guess Judy and Carol knew what they were talking about." She said to herself.

It's too bad that Judy and Tracy's friendship ended right after Tracy moved in with Martin because now she doesn't even have a friend to turn to.

Once breakfast was ready, Tina sent her husband to get Tracy. Ron walked down the long narrow hallway to the door on the left. He knocked a couple of times before entering after entering he didn't see Tracy anywhere but he heard the sound of the shower running. Ron stood there for a second or two and debated if he should knock on the door, but just then the water stopped and a couple minutes later, the door opened and there stood Tracy naked. Ron stood there speechless while his eyes were glued to her large breast and the way her nipples looked. Tracy noticed how Ron was checking her out and how handsome he looked. She could not believe that a man his age could get her off balance but he did. Ron stood at 6'3 with a muscular build, salt & pepper hair with a mustache and low wavy fade. Tracy guessed Ron was around forty- five or maybe just a little younger than that.

"Oh, I am so sorry." Ron said as he backed out of the room eyes still glued to her breast."

Once Ron was on the outside, he yelled through the door.

"Breakfast is ready, come join us when you're ready."

"Okay, thanks," Tracy said, trying not to giggle.

The look on Ron's face told Tracy that she could easily turn his ass out if she wanted to. "Um... I might have to give Ron a taste of this good pussy and see what it gets me."

Tracy finished dressing as her mind stayed on Ron. Ron was sexy as hell the more she thought about him, the more he intrigued her.

Making her way down the hall to the kitchen, she noticed how uneasy Ron seemed as she walked in. He looked up at her and quickly diverted his gaze to his wife.

"I hope I didn't take too long."

"Oh no, you're just in time."

"Oh my God, I'm starving."

Louise walked over and placed a plate of food in front of Tracy.

"Thank you so much," Tracy said as Louise eyed her suspiciously.

Louise noticed how she walked in the room with her sheer blouse on showing her breast as she eyed the Mr. Why did she even bothered to wear a blouse. Louise thought to herself.

"Again, I want to thank you guys for everything you're doing for me."

Louise turned back to look at Tracy with a hard gaze. She didn't trust Tracy after Trina told her what had happened and she especially didn't trust her around Mr. Patterson.

"Some people just love to bring in trash off the street," Louise said low enough so no one could hear.

Just then, Tracy looked up to see Louise staring at her with a mean look on her face. "What the fuck is her problem." Tracy thought to herself.

Tracy continued to eat breakfast as she blocked out the conversation that was going on between Ron and Trina. She wondered how she ended up this way. How could I have been so stupid to let myself be blinded by love? Tracy focused her attention back to Ron when she caught him gazing at her breast. She turned to Trina to see if she had noticed how hard her husband had been staring at her, but she was too busy talking to Louise. Tracy ran one hand across her breast, stopped at her nipple and began to massage it. Tracy slowing looked at Ron to see if he noticed and as she suspected he was watching. She quickly looked at

Trina who was still busy talking to Louise. Tracy dipped her finger into the bowl of honey and brought it to her mouth, she began to lick each side as if she was licking a big dick before inserting it into her mouth. She looked at Ron with his mouth wide open and tongue hanging out. Tracy winked at Ron and grinned.

"Tracy, why don't you tell us about yourself," Trina asked.

"Well, there's nothing much to tell. I was given up for adoption when I was one day old and was raised by four sets of foster parents. I'm an only child and I have no living relatives that I know. I worked for Anthem for five years before I allowed that creep Martin to talk me into quitting. That's about it."

"What about you guys. How long have you been married and do you have any children?"

"Ron and I have been married for twenty years and we don't have any children."

"That's nice that you guys have been married for so long."

Ron was quiet the entire time. He was trying his best to keep his eyes to himself.

"What about you Ron tell me something about yourself?"

"What do you want to know?"

"How old are you if you don't mind me asking?"

"No, I don't mind. I don't get caught up in that age thing. I'm 42 years young." Ron joked.

"Okay, what do you like to do in your spare time?" Before he could answer, Louise chimed in, "that has nothing to do with the price of tea in China. I don't see the point in your questions."

"You don't see my point because I am not asking you these questions. I asked Ron Patterson."

"I know who you asked, but your concerns should be on finding a job and getting your own place. That's all."

"I'm sorry you're right," Tracy said as the tears formed in her eyes. Tracy stood up and excused herself from the table.

"Louise, why are you being so rude to our guest?" Ron asked after Tracy had left the room.

"Because I don't like her, she's nothing but trouble."

"Do you know her?" Ron asked.

"No, I don't, but I can sense trouble from her."

"That's nonsense and you know it. You know you owe her an apology."

Louise looked at Trina and Trina shook her head.

"Okay, I will apologize in my own time."

"I don't care when you do it, I just want you to apologize to her."

"I will," Louise said as she exited the kitchen and made her way down to the other end of the hall where her room was.

CHAPTER FIVE

Tracy sat on the side of the bed and broke down. She tried to play the strong person, but deep down inside she was broken. She loved Martin with all her heart, but in the end, he betrayed her. All at once, the tears begin to fall uncontrollably.

She sat in the guest room for hours trying to pull herself together and figure out what she was going to do with her life. She thought about calling her old boss to ask for her job back, but she couldn't. Tracy knew she couldn't face Judy and the other women in the department. Tracy thought about leaving town to get a new start, but there was one little problem, she had no money. She was busy trying to figure things out when she heard a knock at the door.

"Come in."

Tracy was expecting to see Trina or Louise but was surprised when Ron walked through the door.

"Hey you, how are doing?"

"I'm just trying to figure things out. I need a job and I need one fast."

"How about I talk to my HR representative and see what she has available. I'm pretty sure she can find something for you."

"That would be wonderful Ron."

"I came to apologize to you for the way Louise acted towards you. I told her to apologize to you."

"Oh, that's okay. There's no need for an apology. She's right, I need to focus on other things."

Ron moved closer to Tracy and with his finger, he lifted her chin up.

"Keep your head up things will get better, I promise."

Tracy looked up at Ron, and out of nowhere, Ron moved closer to Tracy and before they both knew it they were kissing. Ron ran his tongue alongside her lips outlining her lips with his tongue once he finished he made his way back inside of her mouth as his hand rubbed the nipple of her breast until it became hard. Tracy pushed Ron back onto the bed, climbed on top, and straddled him. The two were going at it hot and heavy when they heard a knock at the door. Tracy jumped up, fixed her clothes while Ron ran and hid in the bathroom.

"Come in."

Louise walked in.

"I just came to apologize for my behavior earlier, it was uncalled for and I'm sorry. Are you okay?" Louise asked, seeing how puzzled Tracy looked.

"Oh, I'm fine. Just trying to get my head together, that's all."

"Well, like I said I just came to apologize," Louise said as she walked out of the room closing the door behind her. Louise stood outside the door, she could have sworn she smelled Ron's cologne in the room. She shook it off and made her way down the hall to the kitchen.

After Louise left, Tracy walked over to the bathroom, stuck her head in and told Ron that the coast was clear.

"That was a close call," Ron said as he wiped the sweat from his forehead.

"But it was worth it," Tracy said.

Ron pulled Tracy to him and kissed her on the lips.

"I got to get out of here."

The next couple of days Ron tried his best to avoid Tracy as much as possible and if he was in the same room with her, he made sure Trina or Louise was around. Tracy played it cool around Ron, but deep down inside she knew he wanted her he was just afraid of getting caught. Ron kept his word and talk to his HR rep and she was able to find employment for Tracy. The pay wasn't what she wanted, but it was better than nothing. Tracy still could not afford to move out on her own just yet, but the Patterson's were okay with that. Trina actually enjoyed having Tracy around, she was like a daughter that Trina never had. They would have their spa day, every other Saturday after they finished shopping. Their Sunday dinners were always spent together out on the deck and for the most part, Tracy and Louise got along pretty good they were like one big happy family until Louise walked in on Ron and Tracy in the kitchen one night. She eased out of the kitchen without being seen as she didn't want to know what was going to happen between the two and ever since then, she had been a little distant toward Tracy.

Ron awoke from his sleep. He sat on the side of his bed and ran his hand across his face. He looked off into space as he tried his best to remember his dream. The dream had him horny as hell. He wanted to go to the bathroom and Jack off but he decided against it. He looked back at his wife who was knocked out so he decided to let her sleep. Ron eased out the bed, slid his house slippers on, and made his way downstairs to the kitchen. Ron walked over to the refrigerator and pulled out the leftovers from dinner. He walked over to the cabinet, pulled out a plate, put some food onto the plate, and placed it in the microwave. He put the remaining food back and grabbed him a can of Pepsi.

Tracy tossed and turned for most of the night. She had such a hard time falling asleep that she decided to get up. She walked over and turned the television on. Tracy flicked through several channels until she came to the television series Power. This brought memories back to when she and Martin would get together and watch Power together. This was one of his favorite shows. They would make several dishes and sit, eat and watch the series. Just thinking about the food made Tracy hungry. Tracy threw back the covers, got up and made her way down the hall to the kitchen where she found Ron standing at the sink waiting for the microwave to buzz.

"I guess we both had the same idea."

Ron looked up to see Tracy standing there in her tee shirt.

"Yeah, I guess so." Ron laughed a nervous laugh.

Ron tried his best not to look at the shapely legs that stood before him and the firm breast that oozed out of the tee shirt.

Tracy made her way further into the kitchen. She walked over to the refrigerator. She opened the door, bent over giving Ron an eye full and removed the pan of food. Tracy placed the pan on top of the stove and moved over to the cabinet to grab a plate. When Tracy bent over the thickness of her pussy lips had Ron on full drive, he felt his penis increase just at the sight of it. Sweat beads started forming on Ron's forehead and his mouth was dry that each time he tried to swallow it was difficult.

"Shit."

Tracy turned around and looked at Ron.

"Did you say something?"

"Not a word."

Ron tried to hide the bulge in his pants when the microwave buzzer went off, Ron was thankful for the distraction. Ron inhaled his food and quickly made his way back to his room. Tracy got a kid out of tormenting Ron she loved seeing him so nervous whenever they were alone

The following week, Trina and some of her girlfriends were taking a trip to Los Angeles to the beach house in Hermosa Beach. Tracy was very disappointed that Trina didn't ask her to go. Trina was taking Louise along to cook their meals for them and decided to leave her and Ron behind to fend for themselves.

Tracy was in her room pouting when she heard a knock at her door. Tracy opened the door to find Trina and Louise standing there.

"Hey, Tracy I just wanted to let you know that Louise and I are heading out for the airport. There's enough food to last you guys for two weeks. If you need anything I can be reached at this number or on my cell." Trina hands Tracy a card with the phone number to the beach house. "Oh, and Ron should be home shortly. I'll see you in two weeks."

"Okay. You guys have fun and call us when you get there."

Tracy stood in the door and watched as Trina and Louise drove off. She only wished she could have been traveling with them. Ever since Martin took her to the beach house, she had fallen in love with it.

Once they were out of sight, she closed the door and headed for the kitchen. Tracy was bored and since she and Judy were no longer friends, she didn't have any girlfriends to hang out with.   Tracy made her way out onto the deck and took a seat. Sitting on the deck made her feel so at ease. She could sit there all day and daydream about how she wanted her life to be.

Ron walked through the door after hanging up with Trina. He doesn't feel comfortable staying in the house with Tracy while Trina was away, but he would make the best of it. He was going to make sure that they didn't have any more moments like they had had that time in her bedroom, but if Ron was honest with himself he would admit that he enjoyed every bit of it. Ron enjoyed seeing her that night in the kitchen when she bent over giving him a glimpse of herself.

"Down boy down," Ron said as he felt himself starting to rise.

Ron headed upstairs to his bedroom to change his clothes. He laid his briefcase down in the corner, kicked his shoes off and started undressing when he heard music coming from the outside. He walked over to his balcony doors and opened them he could hear the music louder. Ron stepped out onto the balcony when he saw Tracy sitting there listening to music with a glass of wine. He was thinking about doing the same thing, but now he has reservations about it.

Ron made his way downstairs to the deck, but when he got there, Tracy was gone so Ron took a seat and relaxed as he sipped on his drink. He listened to the music and thought about how relaxing this was when Tracy stood in the doorway with her bikini on.

"Hello, Ron," Tracy said as she made her way to the swimming pool.

"Why don't you come and join me?" Ron knew this was a bad idea, but right now, he couldn't resist the offer.

Ron hesitated as he watched Tracy dive into the pool. He watched her do several laps before removing his clothes and hopped in butt ass naked.

Tracy swam up to Ron and stood right in front of him.

"I see I have you all to myself for two weeks," Tracy said and then swam away.

Ron followed pursuit and caught up with her. "What do you mean you have me all to yourself?"

"All right, you can cut the bullshit, Ron. I know you want to fuck me. I know you want to taste my sweet pussy just like I want to fuck the shit out of you."

Ron was stunned, but he couldn't lie he wanted her bad and especially since that night in the kitchen.

"Come here, Tracy."

"What do you want Ron?" Tracy asked as she back away.

"Why don't you come see what I want?"

"No! If you want me, come and get me." Tracy said playfully as she swam away.

"If I have to come and get you, I guarantee you, you won't like what I'm going to do to you."

"Oh really, I'll just take my chances," Tracy said as she continued to swim.

Ron chased Tracy in the pool for about two minutes before he was able to catch her.

"Oh," Tracy screamed as Ron grabbed a hold of her and forced her back up against the wall of the swimming pool. Tracy wrapped her legs around Ron's waist as he cuffed her butt under the water. She threw her arms around Ron's neck as he moved closer to kiss her. After several minutes, Ron broke the kiss and removed the top of her bikini. He brought his mouth down on one breast as his tongue did its magic.

"Oh, Ron honey, that turns me on."

"That's what I'm trying to do. I want you and I want you bad. I want to fuck your brains out."

"Have you ever fucked your wife in the pool?"

"No Trina would never do anything like that."

"Her loss."

Tracy said as she guided his dick to her pussy and inserted it inside of her.

"Damn you feel so good," Ron said as he moved deeper inside of Tracy.

"Damn you ain't bad at all for an old man."

"Old man, I got your old man right here inside you."

"And I love it."

Before he released himself, Ron pulled out and took Tracy by the hand. He helped her out of the pool, laid her down beside the pool, and buried himself between her legs.

"Damn Ron you got skills for an old man."

"I told you I got your old man. I love eating pussy but Trina won't let me do that."

"Her loss again."

Tracy said as she pulled Ron's head closer.

"Damn baby eat that pussy good."

Tracy pulled Ron from between her legs and motioned for him to lie on his back. Tracy grabbed a hold of his penis and began licking the side of it like she was licking a Popsicle and then she put the head in her mouth and gradually inched more of him inside of her mouth. She cuffed Ron's ass with her hands and moved his body up and down as his penis went in and out of her mouth.

"Oh shit Tracy. Girl you are going to make me come."

Tracy removed his penis from her mouth and started licking and blowing on his balls.

"Oh shit." Was all Ron could say.

Within minutes, Tracy was on top of Ron riding the hell out of him. Her pussy was so good, she had Ron singing songs."

"Come with me, baby." Tracy yelled as she rode Ron like she was riding a bull.

Seconds later the two lay there, they forgot all about being outside and about the nosy neighbors.

CHAPTER SIX

THE BEACH HOUSE

Trina and her girls arrived at the beach house later that evening. They arrived just as the sun began to set. This was the first time that her friends had been to the beach home.

"Trina this is lovely," Renee said. How come this is the first time that you have asked us to come here?"

"I know. She's been keeping this a secret from us."

"No, I haven't. If I remember correctly, Ron and I invited Gloria and her husband here last year when we came, but you guys had to attend Tommy's graduation. And as for as you Renee, you were too busy with you know who to go anywhere without him so I don't want to hear any crap from the two of you."

"Why don't you ladies stop running your mouth and put your stuff up so we can go get something to eat. I am starving. That mess they served on the plane was garbage." Louise said to the women.

Laughter filled the room. "I guess we heard that."

"Okay, Ms. Louise we're going to get you something to eat," Trina promised.

"You're not like yourself when you're hungry." Gloria joked and they all laughed.

The women went into their rooms and carried their belongings with them. Gloria, Trina, and Louise all had a view of the Pacific Ocean. Renee, on the other hand, had a view of all the beautiful beach homes.

"Oh my God! I could stay here forever." Gloria said as she pulled open the balcony doors.

"Renee, come here," Gloria yelled. "You have got to see this view."

"Don't rub it in," Renee said as she walked in. "I guess I can't be mad you won your room fair and square."

Trina knew the room situation would be a big problem for Gloria and Renee so she had Louise, Gloria and Renee all pull numbers to see who would get the rooms that had the ocean view. She had been around these women long enough to know how they were. They were always competing with each other.

Once the women took their luggage to their room and met back in the living room area, they decided on the same restaurant that Martin and Tracy visited. They enjoyed the music and the food while looking out into the ocean.

"This is so relaxing," Louise said.

"I know. I can't believe you only come here once a year."

"And who told you I only come here once a year?" Trina laughed.

"Oops, I just thought you came here once a year. You never mentioned to us about coming any other time."

"Maybe it's because I come here without Ron."

"Girl shut up," Renee said.

"What are you trying to say, Trina?" Gloria asked.

"That I come here more than once a year just not with Ron."

"Speaking of Ron how could you leave your fine ass husband at home with your house guest? You know you're asking for trouble, don't you?"

"I tried to tell her that Tracy ain't nothing but trouble." Louise chimed in.

"Who does that? Who leaves their husband alone for two weeks with a pretty young house guest?" Renee asked.

"Hey, if you want to give your husband away, you can send him my way."

"Gloria I see you are full of jokes tonight," Trina said.

"I'm not joking, when you get home, you probably won't have a husband. All I'm saying is if you wanted to get rid of Ron I would have definitely taken him off your hands."

"So why did you guys allow her to live with you after what she and Martin did?"

"Well, she had no knowledge of anything. She believed everything Martin told her. She quit her job and gave up her apartment so when we came back from Paris and found her in our bed and found out what Martin had done, I felt sorry for her because she had no family and nowhere to go. Ron wanted to call the police and throw her out, but I convinced him to allow her to stay until she's able to move out on her own."

"So you guys haven't heard or seen Martin's luscious ass?"

"Gloria, what is it with you? Do you need some dick in your life?"

Trina laughed at Gloria and Renee, but she had to agree with Gloria about Martin because he was gorgeous and sexy as hell and from what she knew Martin had a big thick ass dick and knows how to work it.

"Trina, I have noticed that whenever someone mentions Martin's name you have the biggest smile on your face or you get agitated when we joke about his good looks?"

"Girl please." Trina tried to play if off, but what they don't know is that Trina and Martin were having an affair. So when she caught him in bed with the housekeeper, she was so pissed that she fired him and then turned around and fired Calvin because he knew this had been going on for months and never bothered to tell her. Calvin knew of the relationship that Martin and she had because he brought them together.

About a year ago, Martin had been telling Calvin that he was digging Trina and for months, Calvin kept telling him to leave it alone before he lost his job, but when Martin continued to express his feeling about Trina, Calvin brought it to Trina's attention. Trina was flattered she never looked at Martin in that way until then. One thing led to another and they started fucking and had been for over a year. Trina had actually fallen in love with Martin and was planning to leave her husband for him, but after thinking about what she had to lose, she reconsidered her decision and that was why Martin started sleeping with the housekeeper in her bed.

Trina was busy listening to Gloria and Renee talk about Martin when her phone rang.

"Hello, hello." Then the line went dead. Trina threw her phone back in her purse and just as she did, it rung again.

"Hello."

"Hey, sexy."

Trina was shocked and pissed at the same time. She excused herself from the table before speaking.

"How dare you call me after the shit you have pulled."

"Aw, baby don't be mad. You know I still love you."

"Do you still love me?"

"Go to hell," Trina said before hanging up. She then put her phone on silent mode and placed it back in her purse. When Trina returned to the table, the women could tell she was upset.

"Is everything okay?" Louise asked.

"Yes, everything's fine."

"You have never been a good liar," Renee said.

"Girl I am fine. I promise."

"Was that Ron?" Gloria asked.

"No, it wasn't."

"Um, someone is doing something behind their husbands back."

Trina gave Renee the meanest look.

"Don't you dare start any rumors, Renee."

"Aren't we touchy?"

Just then, the waiter showed up with their food and drinks.

"Not only is this place heaven, but the food is good as well."

"I know I love to come here, look out into the ocean and feed my face."

"If you guys ever decide to sell this place, let me know so I can buy it from you."

"Buy it with what?" Renee asked.

Trina and Louise laughed.

"I have a little money put up and I know Ron and Trina would give me a good deal."

"Sorry, but I am not selling my beach home. You better go ahead and get your own. There are several beach homes up for sale around here. We could be neighbors."

"Right, in her fucking dreams," Renee said as she laughed.

"Renee stop being such a hater."

"Gloria you know I am just joking with you. We all know that rich old man left you a fortune."

By the time the women made it back to the beach home, they were all drunk except for Louise. She made sure that women got home safe.

"Man, I could use Martin's ass right now," Gloria said.

"Girl please, what makes you think he would have anything to do with you?" Trina asked.

Gloria and Renee looked at Trina. Trina continued walking up the stairs to her room. She was fed up with the women and all their questions. The women, on the other hand, knew something was up with Trina and Martin they just didn't know what.

"Good night ladies," Trina said as she shut her door. As soon as Trina shut her door, she began stripping her clothes off. She made way to the French doors and open them, allowing the nice warm breeze to enter. Hearing the ocean always put her at ease. She remembered when she would spend nights sleeping on the balcony in the nude and making love to her lover. She would do anything to get those days back.

He stood outside the beach house and waited for all the lights in the beach house to go out before he entered. He walked quietly up the walkway to the stairs that led to one of the rooms in the beach house. As he suspected the doors were wide open, He eased his way inside the room and noticed that the bed was empty, but heard the water from the shower running. He quickly removed his clothes and made his way to the bathroom. He opened the door slowly and made his way inside. The stranger stood there for a minute admiring the silhouette of a woman's body. He began to pull on his dick getting it hard and ready for what he was about to do. The stranger entered the shower from the back. Trina's back was now facing him when all of a sudden she felt a hard body against her and a hand across her mouth. She tried to scream, but she couldn't, and as she turned to face him the smile that she had on her face said it all.

"Aw, so you do miss me."

"What are you doing here?" She asked, trying to hide her excitement.

"Oh, do you want me to leave. I can leave and go to another room in this house that I know would want this here." He pointed to his penis.

"You make me sick." She said as she rolled her eyes.

"Hey, it's the truth."

"You are such a whore."

"I'm your whore aren't I?"

Trina moved closer to him and laid her head against his chest. She tried to fight the feelings that stirred up inside of her, but she couldn't, she was still in love with him.

"Why are you doing this to me?"

"I love you Trina and I want you to be my wife."

"You know that's impossible." She said as the tears started to fall.

"Don't cry baby just trust me, I have a plan that will allow you to be my wife and for you not to lose anything. Trust me, it's already in motion."

"What are you talking about Martin?"

"I can't tell you just yet. Give me two weeks. When you return to Indiana, I will fill you in on everything.

"Well, until then I want you to fuck the hell out of me Mr. Jackson."

"I thought you would never ask."

Martin turned around to turn off the shower and carried Trina to the bed. He laid her down in the middle of the bed and told her to spread her legs.

"I'm doing what I want to do to you tonight." Trina did not believe in oral sex so Martin was never able to please her orally, but that will change tonight.

"Well before you get started you might want to lock my bedroom door."

After locking the door, Martin stood at the foot of the bed and began to crawl toward Trina until he reached her inner thighs.

"Can I do what I want to do?"

Trina shook her head yes. Martin began kissing her inner thighs. He moved slowly up her body until he came to her pussy. He opened the folds of her pussy and slowly touched her clit with his tongue. The feeling that came over Trina caused her to jump.

"Just relax baby, I got this."

"Oh, Martin what are you going to do to me."

"I'm going to make you feel real good."

Martin touched her again with his tongue. This time he applied more pressure. He began to lick her from the top of her clit to the end of her clit and then he made his way down to her hole where he stuck his tongue in and out and all around and back to her clit. Trina thought she would lose her mind. The feeling was just too much for her.

"Are you okay babe?"

"Martin that feels so damn good. Baby, please don't stop."

Martin laughed as he went back to work.

"I won't stop I am here to please you."

When Martin was finished, Trina had come three times. Now it was his time to come. He climbed on top of Trina and entered her slowly. He inserted the head first giving her time to adjust to it and then he inserted the rest of himself. Martin slowly moved in and out deeper and deeper and then he turned her over on her stomach and took her from the back. Martin had Trina on all fours while he banged the hell out of her.

"Whose pussy is it?"

"It's yours."

"It's whose?"
"It's yours."
"Say my name baby."
"It's yours, Martin."

Early that morning Trina reached over to hug Martin, but he was gone. He was nowhere in sight. There was no trace of Martin anywhere.

Trina grabbed her robe and made her way into the hallway. Her door was already unlocked, but she thought Martin had locked it last night. She was drunk last night so she started to believe she imagined the entire episode.

Trina continued downstairs where the women greeted her. They were all dressed and ready to go.

"It's about time you got up?" Gloria said.

"What time is it?"

"It's one in the afternoon."

"Are you serious? Why didn't anyone wake me earlier?"

"I was just about to," Renee said.

"Here have a seat why I warm up your breakfast," Louise told Trina.

"What do you guys want to do today?" Trina asked.

"You already know what I want to do. I want to shop." Gloria said.

"Take us to the Alley."

"The Alley it is. Let me finish breakfast and then I will go up and get dressed."

CHAPTER SEVEN

The last couple of days had been great for Ron and Tracy. They fucked like bunny rabbits. Ron called off work three days in a row just to spend time with Tracy since her department had shut down for the week due to plumbing problems. Ron took Tracy to Cincinnati to visit the Cincinnati Zoo and to do some shopping. He spent over three thousand dollars on her. Tracy had Ron's nose wide open. He had never experienced the sex that he shared with Tracy and her youthfulness made Martin feel young at heart. Tracy was spontaneous, but with Trina, everything had to be planned out weeks in advance.

"Ron I have had the best time today," Tracy said as she kissed Ron and grabbed him between the legs. I want to fuck right now."

"Right here?"

"Yes, right here. Right here in the parking lot of the Cincinnati Zoo."

"What if we get caught?"

"We won't just do as I say. Get out and get in the back and lay down and I will crawl over the seat."

"You're serious aren't you?"

Ron saw the look on her face, got out of the car and hopped in the back. Just as she said, she crawled over the seat and position herself on top of Ron. Ron pulled her thong down and she unbuckled his belt, unfastened his pants and pulled his boxers down. She moved down to his dick, grabbed a hold of it and licked the head, then the side before taking him into her mouth. Ron moaned as the feeling made his toes curl. Once he was where she wanted him and her pussy started to throb, she straddled him, placed him inside of her and rode him for dear life until they both came.

"Damn babe I don't know if I will be able to drive home after this."

"We can always get a hotel."

"Yeah, I guess you're right."

Ron drove to the closest Hotel and got a room for the night. Ron was exhausted. He wanted to relax in the hotel and get room service, but Tracy wasn't ready to call it a night. It was only a little after six in the evening.

"Ron, are you serious. It's still early."

"What do you want to do?"

"I want to go someplace where we can get some food and listen to some jazz."

"Damn, I'm tired. Let me hop in the shower and see if that helps."

"You want me to join you?"

"If you do, we definitely won't be leaving this room tonight."

"Well, let me hop in first and you can take a quick nap." Tracy was in the shower for about fifteen minutes and another ten minutes, making herself presentable and trying to give Ron time to rest because what she had in store for him was going to drive his ass crazy.

"Okay, it's all yours," Tracy said waking Ron from his nap. "I've changed my mind. I want to stay in and order room service. What would you like? I'm going to order us some wine as well.

"Whatever you get will be fine with me," Ron said as he made his way into the bathroom.

Tracy turned the television on in search of the music channel. She wanted to hear some soft Jazz to set the tone for what she had in store for Ron. Room service brought up the wine right away. She dimmed the lights and opened the door to their balcony. She was trying to relive the time she shared with Martin at the beach house.

Twenty minutes later, Ron emerged from the bathroom in only his towel. When he entered the bedroom, he found Tracy in the middle of the bed with a glass of wine in one hand and the other hand was rubbing away at her clit. Her legs were wide open, giving him a great view.

"I already poured you a drink. I want you to have a seat in the chair right there."

Ron sat at the foot of the bed in a chair while Tracy continued to please herself as Ron watched. It turned him on watching her please herself. He wanted to remove her hand and replace it with his tongue, but she told him he was not allowed to touch he could only observe until she was ready for him. He continued to watch her stroke her clit and insert her fingers in and out of her pussy.

"Oh, daddy this feels so damn good." Tracy moaned.
By this time, Ron was drooling at the mouth. He wanted to fuck the shit out of her.

"Oh baby daddy is going to fuck you real good," Ron said as he stroked himself.
Tracy looked at him. "You're not playing by the rules, Ron. You can't touch me or yourself. I want to make your body ache from watching and not being able to touch."

"Ron I want you to try to imagine your tongue running up and down my clit. Imagine me licking the head of your dick and taking you in my mouth and making you disappear like magic. Imagine me licking your balls and you inserting your tongue inside me and then your dick and then me riding you into ecstasy. Can you imagine that baby?"

"Baby please don't do this to me." Ron pleaded his voice husky and full of want. I need you right now."
Tracy stopped and placed her wine on the nightstand. She scooted her way down to Ron with her legs spread wide open. "Eat me, baby."
Ron almost dropped his drink he was in such a hurry to get to the pussy, but before he could eat, there was a knock at the door.

"Room service."

"Aw shit," Ron yelled.
After dinner, Tracy and Ron replayed their sex scene over from beginning to the end.

"Tracy turn over I want to fuck you from behind," Ron said as he slowly inserted his penis into her ass.

"No Ron no."

"Just relax Tracy. It will only hurt for a minute."
Ron moved slowly in and out of that ass until the feeling took over and he rammed his dick in and out of her.

"Ron stop please stop." Tracy cried out, but her cries went unheard.

After a minute or so, Ron collapsed on top of Tracy. Tracy was in so much pain that she couldn't move.

"Are you okay, Tracy."

"What the fuck do you think? I told you to stop you were hurting me."

"I'm sorry babe. It felt so damn good that I couldn't stop. I am so sorry."

"Get off of me." Tracy said as she eased off the bed and made her way to the bathroom."

Ron stood talking through the door.

"Tracy I am so sorry. Do you want me to run you a bath? That might help with the pain."

"Get the fuck away from the door and leave me alone."

The next day Tracy was in such a bad mood Ron was afraid to say anything to her. She was quiet at Breakfast and on the way home. Once they made it home, she stayed cooped up in her room.

Ron ran out to the drugstore to get her some medicine for her butt because she asked him to and he made her an ice pack, but other than that, she hadn't said a word to him. That evening he took Tracy some dinner and sat it outside her door. She ate it and placed the tray back outside the door when she was finished. Ron felt bad, but he always enjoyed anal sex, but he was not able to enjoy it with his wife so he tried it with Tracy, big mistake he thought.

The women shopped until they could not shop anymore.

"Hey, let's try another restaurant this evening that is also on the beach. I just love the scenery." Gloria said.

The women walked the boardwalk checking out the different restaurants when they came across the perfect place called Abigaile-Ocean Bar.

"What do you guys think about this place?" Trina asked.

"Let's look at the menu first," Renee said.

"Everything sounds good. I don't know what to choose." Louise said.

"How are you ladies doing this evening? Would any of you care for a drink?" The young handsome waiter asked.

"Yeah, I will have a sex on the beach," Renee said.

"I'll have sex anywhere," Gloria said jokingly.

"You sure are silly girl." Trina and the rest of the women laughed along with the waiter.

After dinner, the women sat there and drank one drink after the other. Louise sat there and shook her head. "You guys are nothing but drunks.

"Louise, I'm not drunk I just a little tipsy. That's all." Trina said, unable to walk a straight line.

"Okay, just keep walking," Louise said

Once they finally made it back to the house. Trina only hoped that she wasn't dreaming about making love to Martin and hoped he would return tonight. She made her way to her room hoped in the shower and half expected him to show up, but he didn't. She lay in bed butt naked with the door to her balcony open, but still no Martin.

Trina was up early that morning. She was thirsty from all the drinking last night so she made her way into the hall heading downstairs when she approached Gloria's room. She thought she heard moaning sounds coming from her room. All sorts of things popped in her head. She moved closer to the door and true enough, she heard what she thought she heard. Fearing the worst, she reached for the door to see if it was open and it was. Trina pushed the door open and as quietly as she could, she walked further into the room where she found Gloria and Martin having sex. She was so shocked all she could do was just stand there. Martin turned around just to see her standing and smiled but never stopped fucking Gloria. Trina was so furious, but she couldn't say anything. Trina backed out of the room, shut the door and ran back to her room where she broke down. She was so angry with Gloria that she stayed in her room for hours. She told them that they were on their own today. Trina wanted to be alone. She wanted to go back home to her husband who truly loved her and only her.

Later that evening, Louise knocked at Trina's door. Trina refused to answer so Louise walked in. "What the hell is going on with you?"

"Louise I am not in the mood for this."

"Did I ask you what you were in the mood for? Now I have known you for years. I can tell when something isn't right. Now, what's going on?"

Louise knew all about Trina and Martin. She pleaded with Trina to leave Martin alone before she lost her husband.

"Early this morning I caught Gloria and Martin having sex."

"What! What was he doing here? I thought you broke that off?"

"I did, but the other night he came to my room and the next night he was with Gloria. I feel so stupid." Trina said as she started crying.

Louise walked over, sat on the bed beside her and hugged her.

"Child, I told you that boy wasn't right, but you wouldn't listen. That man ain't nothing but a whore. You women better start protecting yourself because there's no telling what he's carrying. So are you going to say something to Gloria about it?"

"I can't say anything because he's not my husband."

"Have you spoken to Ron since you've been here?"

"No, I forgot all about him."

"What. You women today are something else when you get back home, you probably won't have a husband."

"Louise don't say that."

"Honey I'm just being realistic about things. I think you should come back when we come back. Were you staying an extra week to be with Martin?"

"Trina looked at her with the saddest eyes."

"Yeah, you need to come back with us."

"Are you hungry?" Louise asked as she sat holding Trina's hand.

"I went to the store while Gloria and Renee were at the beach. I'll bring you something up when dinner's ready."

"Thanks, Louise."

"Do me a favor."

"What."

"Call your husband."

"Okay."

When Louise left, Trina grabbed her phone and dialed Ron's number. Ron answered on the fourth ring.

"What took you so long? Were you busy?"

"And hello to you too."

"I'm sorry. How are you?"

"I'm doing better than you sound. What's going on? Did you and one of the girls get into it?"

"No, we're fine. I don't feel too good."

"Did you have too much to drink?"

"Probably."

Ron laughed.

"What's going on with you and why haven't you called me?"

"Oh, I have been hanging out with Tracy"

"Hanging out? Did you fuck her?"

"Come on Tracy."

"Tracy!"

"I mean Trina."

"If I find out that you been fucking her I will kill the both of you." She yelled and then hung up.

"Aw, I hate men!" She yelled

Louise knocked at the door and came in with dinner. "Did you call?"

"Yes, I called and that fucker is probably fucking Tracy. He's been hanging out with her calling me by her name. I swear I hate men right now."

"I don't want to be the bearer of bad news, but I warned you about her. She ain't right either. That girl is looking for a man with money and your husband definitely has that plus he's handsome."

"Don't say that Louise. You're going to make me fly home tonight."

"If you go I'm going with you."

"Can you ask the girls if they want to stay without us because I'm going back tomorrow?"

"Sure."

Trina was on the phone with the airline when Louise walked back into the room.

"They want to stay."

"Okay, thanks."

"Yes, I would like to change the date of my return flight for Louise James from Friday the 12th to Wednesday the 10th same time if possible and change my flight from Friday the 19th to Wednesday the 10th same time as Louise James."

"Okay, great. Thank you so much."

"Start packing Trina said as she hung up the phone. We leave at the 8 am tomorrow."

That night, Trina was sleeping, but she wasn't in a deep sleep when she heard someone jiggling her balcony door. She eased out of bed, grabbed her stun gun and inched closer to the door. She stood there for a minute and then opened it swiftly.

"What the hell are you doing here?" Startling him.

"Oh shit. You scared the daylights out of me. Martin said as he tried to kiss Trina, but she backed away.

"Now don't be like that babe."

"How dare you come to me after you slept with Gloria this morning. You got me twisted if you think I'm going to fuck you after that. Go to her damn room and stay out of mine. Oh, by the way, I am leaving tomorrow and if I hear of you being here with Gloria, I will turn your ass in. Do I make myself clear?"

"You should be mad at your friend as well. She's the one that's been contacting me to come and fuck her. Does she know about us?"

"Why the fuck would she?"

"I just figure she was trying to make you jealous."

"Jealous, "jealous of what?"

"Oh, it's like that now."

"What are you talking about?"

"Are you saying I'm nothing?"

"Boy, I do not have time for this."

"Boy, I got your boy right here and when you want it, let me know and don't make me wait too long. Boy, shit you tripping."

Martin pulled his dick out.

"What boy has a dick like this and can make women fall in love with it. Huh, you tell me."

Trina looked at his dick. It looked so good. Martin must have noticed how Trina was looking and backed her into the room where he stripped down to his boxers and pushed her down to her knees.

"I want you to learn to do this."

Martin talked her through the process of satisfying him orally.

"Damn baby suck this dick, suck the motherfucking skin off. Martin grabbed the back of Trina's head and moved it back and forth harder and harder.

"Aw baby, there you go. Aw shit, girl you got me Crip walking up in this motherfucker."

Martin pulled away from her. I want you to flick the tip of my shit with your tongue. You know as the songs say flick of the wrist, I want you to have the flick of the tongue. Yeah, that's it. Do it slower, though."

Martin backed away again. "I want to get inside." Martin backed her up to the bed and pushed her backward. He spread her legs with his leg, knelt down, raised her legs up in the air and buried his head in the heavenly.

"Aw Martin baby please." Martin had Trina crying it felt so good to her and before she came, he climbed on top of her and entered her in one swift movement.

"Can a boy make you feel this damn good?"

"No Martin no."

Martin pulled out to lick her juices and began licking her asshole before inserting his tongue inside. He ate that ass out in no time and was back inside of her before she came a second time. Two minutes later, Martin came and busted the best nut ever.

"Damn baby you got me pussy whipped. Ain't nobody pussy better than yours and your head game is going to be off the chain with a little more practice.'

Trina just laid there without saying a word.

"Can I take a shower?"

Shaking her head, Trina laid on the bed not sure what just happened, but whatever it was, she loved the hell out of it. When Martin finished in the bathroom, Trina was sound asleep. He kissed her on the lips and placed a note on the pillow next to her.

CHAPTER EIGHT

Trina's alarm clock went off at 5 am, she reached over for Martin, but all she felt was a note.

Trina
I want you to know that I love and care for you with all my heart and because I can't have you just yet, I am free to fuck anyone I want. You fuck your husband so it's not fair that you get mad when I do the same. Be fair and until you can give yourself to me completely, just know I am fucking.
Love Martin

PS. You got the best pussy ever!

"You son of a bitch. No more Martin." She yelled softly. Trina made her way to the bathroom, she showered quickly, dressed and she and Louise headed out for the airport in no time.

"I am so tired. I didn't sleep well at all last night."

"That's understandable seeing that you have a lot on your mind, but unlike me, I slept like a baby."

"Well, as soon as I get on this plane, I am going to pass out. Don't wake me for anything unless we're getting ready to crash or land."

Louise laughed as she patted Trina's knee.

"You sure have a way of saying things. I'm glad I'm not afraid of flying because if I was I would be scared shitless right now."

"Did you get a visitor last night?"

"No."

"Um… never mind.

"What were you going to say?"

"Nothing I'm just going to sit here and mind my own business. You young folk are something else. In my days, people jumped at a chance to have a husband and if he was wealthy that was a plus, but nowadays, you people take things for granted. You people act like someone owes you something and that you are entitled to the best. Shoot, we had to make do with what we had and we appreciated it all.

"So you think I don't appreciate what I have?"

"No, not really. Don't you know there are plenty of women who would love to have what you have and some of them know they will never get what you have, but you don't seem to appreciate it. I hear you and Ron arguing about sexual things. You need to learn to please your husband sexually if not, someone else will. Sometimes he just wants to go and do things, but since you didn't plan it ahead of time, you won't do it. Now that's not right. The only reason I'm telling you this is that I care about you and I want the best for you. I just hope you don't let him slip through your fingers because I have a bad feeling about Tracy. I don't mean to jinx you or anything, but I bet she has seduced Ron."

"Louise I think you're wrong."

"You can think what you want to think, but when I say something, believe me, it's true or it will come true. Just be careful and start doing more with Ron and for Ron if you know what I mean.

Tracy missed her talks and walks around the neighborhood with Ron. She missed his laughter and his smile.   Tracy walked into the kitchen to find Ron sitting at the table drinking his morning coffee.

"Good morning."

"Oh, so you're speaking to me this morning?"

"Yeah, I'm not mad at you anymore."

"Tracy I'm so sorry about what happened at the hotel. I promise I will never do that again."

"Don't worry about it, Ron. It's all forgotten."

"Would you like to go out and eat?"

"Yes, I am starving."

Ron and Tracy had lunch and afterward, went shopping again.

"I can't believe you still want to shop. Didn't you shop enough in Cincinnati?"

"No, I could shop every day."
Tracy said as she held up a tie that she thought would look good on Ron.

"Hey, Ron do you like this?"

"Let me check that out," Ron said as he held the tie to his chest. Yes, this would look good with my gray suit.
Tracy snatched the tie from Ron.

"I'll buy this for you."

"Now I'll buy it."

"Sorry I beat you to it," Tracy said as she walked up to the cashier.

"Will this be all for you?"

"Yes, thank you."

"So what do you want to do now?" Ron asked.

"Do you need to ask?" Tracy said as she wrapped her arm around Ron's waist.

"Well, let me hurry up and get you home."
Once the two made it home, they left the bags by the front door and headed down the hall to Tracy's room.

"Ron baby, I just love this dick. I could never get enough of it."

"You don't have to worry about that you can have it whenever you want it."

"I want it every day," Tracy said as she straddled Ron. Tracy and Ron were so busy that they never heard Trina and Louise enter the house.

"What are these shopping bags doing here and why is Ron home from work so early?" Trina questioned. Louise shook her head and headed down the hall to her room. She already knew what was up and did not want to get in the middle of their mess.

"Ron," Trina yelled.

"OMG! What is she doing back?" Ron said as he continued to stroke Tracy. "Aw Tracy baby come with me."

Tracy wrapped her legs around Ron tighter and squeezed her pussy tightly around his penis. "Damn baby I can't stop coming," Ron said as he heard Trina's voice again.

Once Ron finished coming, he jumped up, ran around gathering his clothes, ran to the bathroom, and shut the door behind him.

Tracy took her time putting her clothes back on. Once she was finished, she walked out and made her way down the hall to collect her shopping bags. When she turned around, she found Trina standing there with her arms folded.

"Hey, Trina you're back so soon."

"Yeah, not soon enough, I see."

"What do you mean?"

"Have you been fucking my husband Tracy?"

"What! Where is this coming from Trina? You know I would never do you like that."

"Yeah, where is that coming from Ron said as he walked up?"

"Why are you home from work so early?"

"I took a couple of days off."

"And why in the hell would you do that?"

"I don't owe you any explanations about what I do. Why did you take off with your girls and leave me behind?"

Trina looked at Ron. She noticed something different about him, but she couldn't put her finger on it.

"Because I knew you wouldn't take off work to go, but I see you took off work for something or should I say, someone?"

"You can say whatever you what, but don't accuse me of anything until you have proof."

"Tracy do you need help with your bags?"

"No, I can manage, but thanks anyway."

"Tracy I want to apologize for my wife's behavior."

Tracy continued down the hall with her bags without saying anything. At this point, she was furious with Trina. "Yes I'm fucking him and soon he will be mine because you don't deserve him." Tracy thought to herself.

"Oh, I see you side with your side bitch." Trina said as she walked passed Ron."

"It's nice seeing you to Trina and yes, I glad you made it home safely," Ron said sarcastically talking to Trina's back.

Later that evening the tension in the home was so thick you could slice it with a knife. Louise stayed in her room and so did Tracy. Tracy did not want a confrontation with Trina because she was afraid that she would let the cat out the bag.
Ron and Trina sat at the kitchen table eating dinner.

"How was your trip and why did you come back so soon?"
Trina looked up at Ron and gave him an evil look.

"Did I ruin your plans?"

"What plans?"

"You tell me."

"Trina what's going on, since you been back, you have been acting like you got something stuck up your ass."
Trina looked at Ron as if he had three heads. Ron had never talked to her like this before. She was trying to figure out what had gotten into him.

"I leave for a few days and I come back and you're like a totally different man why the change Ron?"

"I'm the same person I was when you left. The thing is you just never paid much attention to me. Why is that Trina? Who was on your mind?"
Just then, Tracy walked in.

"Is that the reason for the change?" Trina asked.
Tracy pretended that she didn't hear what Trina had just said.

"This bitch is going to make me hurt her feelings," Tracy said under her breath.

"Trina, how was your trip?" Tracy asked as she turned to face Trina.

"It was okay. Maybe you can have Ron take you one day."

"Sounds good to me." She tried not to go there, but Trina kept pushing. "Now bitch what?" Tracy thought.

Trina almost had an aneurysm when Tracy made that comment.

Trina stood up.

"Bitch I guess you think since you're fucking my husband now you can disrespect me in my home. You have lost your damn mind."

"Trina I am not having sex with your husband. I don't know why you keep accusing me of doing so. You know what they say the one that accuses is usually the one that's cheating. Now, are you cheating?"

"How dare you question me?"

"Well, are you?" Ron asked.

"Trina how could call our guest out of her name. What has gotten into you?" Ron got up and left the kitchen. He was disgusted with Trina right now.

"Trina, what happened? Where did we go wrong? We were fine before you left now that you're back it's like we're enemies and I don't like it. I think it's best that I find my own place." Tracy said.

"I think it's for the best too," Trina said.

Tracy sat down at the table with her food while Trina left her alone in the kitchen. Trina went to the study to look for Ron. Trina stood in the entryway of the study.

"I hope you know your little bitch has decided it's time to find her own place." Ron never moved an inch nor did he say anything. He continued texting on his phone. What Trina doesn't know is that Tracy had just sent him a text telling him and asked if he could help her find a place. Ron thought this was a good idea. Now they wouldn't have to worry about Trina catching them whenever they wanted to fuck. If Trina is not careful, she may end up alone.

CHAPTER NINE

BEACH HOUSE

Gloria was glad to know that Trina and Louise had left. Now she only had to make sure Renee doesn't find out about her and Martin. Martin had phoned Gloria earlier and told her to meet him at three so now she had to find a way to get rid of Renee or sneak off, but Renee was acting like a hawk everywhere Gloria went Renee was right there.

"She needs to sit her cockblocking ass down somewhere." Gloria thought to herself.

"So what are we going to do?" Renee asked.

"You can do whatever you want."

"I thought we would do something together."

"No, not today I 'm just relaxing today."

"Well, I guess I'll go to the beach," Renee said.

"I hope you have a good time at the beach."

Gloria couldn't wait to get rid of her. Martin had been waiting for at least 20 minutes she just hoped he hadn't left. Gloria rushed out the side door and almost ran to her meeting place to meet with Martin. As she came upon their meeting place, she saw Martin standing looking handsome as ever.

"Hey, Handsome." She said as she sneaked up behind him.

"Hey, baby doll," Martin said as he pulled Gloria to him and kissed her on the lips. "For a minute, I thought you stood me up."

"Oh, I had to get rid of Renee's ass. She followed me around like a hawk.

Martin Laughed.

"Well, I'm glad you got rid of her. So what would you like to do?"

"I don't care just as long as I'm with you."

"Okay, let's take a stroll and you can tell me more about Gloria. You know I was very surprised when you called me last week. How did you get my number?"

"I ran into Calvin one day last week and I mentioned to him that I had some work for you. I lied, but he didn't need to know it."

"Trust me, he knew you wanted the D."
Gloria swatted at Martin.

"You women think you're slick, but you're really not. You would be surprised at the excuses women come up with just to get with me. I have heard it all."

"So do you sleep with a lot of women?"

"No I might get my dick sucked by a lot of women, but no, I am picky about who I sleep with."

"Do you eat pussy often?"
Martin chuckled.

"Why you ask me that?"

"Because I want to know."

"Yes, I do that often. Like the Weeknd said, I can make the pussy rain often. Often, often girl I do this often make that pussy poppin do it how I want it, often."

"You are so silly."
They both laughed.

"Well, you asked and I cannot tell a lie."

"Okay, I have a question for you and I want you to be honest. Are you sleeping with Trina?"
Martin smiled.

"Why are you asking me about her and knowing she's married? The one thing that I will not do is to tell a married women's business whether I'm sleeping with them or not. You could destroy a person's life by telling people business like that. I don't fuck and tell just like I would never tell anyone that I'm hitting this."
Martin rubbed his hand between Gloria's thighs touching her pussy and pulling her close to him kissing her on the lips

"I want to fuck." He whispered in her ear.

"I do too. I want you buried between my legs."

"What are we waiting for?"

"Let's go. We have to make sure Renee doesn't see us."

Martin and Gloria headed back to the beach house while Renee was at the beach. They made their way up the stairs looking around trying not to get caught.

"Damn, I feel like I'm an FBI agent or a damn burglar sneaking around and shit."

Gloria laughed. "You are so stupid."

"I'm serious."

Once they made it inside the room, Gloria felt relieved. There was no way she wanted the news of her sleeping with Martin getting back to Trina because she had a feeling that Martin and Trina were sleeping with each other she just couldn't prove it.

After the two finished sexing, they both laid passed out from exhaustion. Gloria awoke to the sound of Renee yelling and knocking at her door.

"Renee, what is it?" She said as she slightly opened the door.

"What are you doing?" Renee asked.

"I was sleep until I was rudely awakened."

"What are we doing for dinner?"

"Damn girl, can't you do something on your own? I'm going back to bed." Gloria said as she shut the door in Renee's face.

Gloria hopped back in bed with Martin and cuddled up with him and the two slept for another two hours.

Hours later, Martin looked at the clock as his stomach growled.

"Man I'm hungry," Martin said as he turned over to wake Gloria up.

"Hey, babe are you hungry?"

"Starving."

"Let's go out and eat."

Martin and Gloria showered, dressed and sneaked out the house and made their way down the boardwalk to one of the restaurants hoping that they did not run into Renee.

After dinner, Martin and Gloria took another walk down the boardwalk holding hands.

"I love it out here. I wish I could buy me a beach house out her. I wouldn't do what Trina and Ron do. I would leave Indiana behind and make a life out here for myself."

"What would you do?"

"I don't know, but I would find something to do and move out here."

"Let's go sit closer to the water," Martin suggested. Martin and Gloria sat on the beach talking, cuddling, and eventually fell asleep in each other's arms until the sun came up.

Gloria opened her eyes and looked around at her surroundings before looking up at Martin whose eyes were on her.

"Are you okay?" Martin asked, seeing the puzzled look on Gloria's face.

"Oh, shit the sun is coming up. Let's go back to the room."

"Lead the way," Martin said.

The next day Ron showered, dressed and headed downstairs when Trina stopped him.

"Where are you going?"

"Tracy asked me if I would help her find an apartment today."

"You're kidding me, right?"

"No, why would I?"

"Ron if you leave this house with her, don't bother coming back. Matter of fact, I want her ass out of here today so you can help her with her belongings."

"Come on Trina stop being so childish. You know damn well she cannot find an apartment this quick."

"That's not my fucking problem."

"If you need me, you know where I am."

"I am warning you, Ron, if you step one foot out of this house."

"Don't you dare warn or threaten me. This is just as much my home as it is yours and the way I see it, I'm the one paying all the bills around anyway. If you have a problem with what's going on, I suggest you find a place to stay. Now that I think of it, Tracy can stay here as long as she wants. It was your idea in the beginning and now because you got a bug up your ass you want to throw her out now, that's not going to happen."

"So you're siding with her over me?"

"I'm not siding with anyone. Right is right, wrong is wrong and you are wrong and you know it. You come home after leaving me behind and starting throwing around accusations about us sleeping with each other. What I don't understand is why are you worried about me sleeping with someone when you won't even sleep with me. Do your damn job and then you wouldn't have to be threatened by a young beautiful woman."

Ron and Trina continued arguing outside the bedroom in the hall where Louise and Tracy could hear. Tracy was amazed that Ron took her side. She knew then that Ron was slowly falling in love with her. Now she just had to find a way to make him divorce Trina. It was clear to everyone that knew the couple, that Trina took advantage of Ron's kindness. Tracy wasn't even sure Trina even loved Ron anymore. She loved the luxuries that Ron gave her, but that was getting ready to end.

"Fuck you and Tracy, if you want that homewrecker, then carry the fuck on," Trina said as she walked back into the bedroom and slammed the door behind her.

Trina was fed up with Ron. She was ready for a divorce so she could be with the man she truly loved, Martin.

Ron walked downstairs where he found Tracy standing.

"Let's get out of here," Ron said to Tracy as he escorted her out the front door.

"I am so sorry that you and Louise had to hear us. I am so sick of her right now. I wish she would file for a divorce."

"Why don't you do it? Then we won't have to sneak around."

"I never wanted my marriage to ever end because of another women, but I can only take so much. To be honest, our marriage ended years ago we just continued to go

through the motion. I have had my suspicions about Trina stepping out on me, but I ignored them. I believe she was sleeping with Martin, I just couldn't prove it."
Tracy's mouth dropped open.

"Are you serious?"

"Oh yeah, I noticed how he looked at her and I noticed how giddy she would get when he was around, but I never said anything or accused her of sleeping with him. I think she allowed you to stay because she wanted to make sure the two of you didn't see each other anymore. She wanted to keep tabs on you."

"I can't believe her."

"Believe it. People think she's a saint, but she's not. She's a fucking devil in disguise."

"Ron, where are we going?"

"I don't know I just had to get out of the house and I wanted to spend some time alone with you. Is that okay?"

"Yes. Why don't we go to the park and have a picnic. We could stop at the store and pick up some items and just enjoy the day talking."

"That sounds like a plan."

Louise knocked at Trina's door. She heard the argument between Ron and Trina and wanted to make sure Trina was okay. She knew this was going to happen because Trina didn't give Ron any attention and when a man's wife doesn't give him any attention and she doesn't take care of his needs, he will find it elsewhere. Ron didn't have to search far to find that attention.
Trina heard the knock at the door and knew it was Louise. Louise was like an aunt to her. She loved Louise with all her heart, but today, she was not in the mood to hear I told you so from Louise.
Trina took small steps toward the door. She was hurt not only by Ron but also by Martin from sleeping with Gloria. She found out that Martin was still in LA probably with Gloria she thought.

Trina opened the door to find Louise standing there as she expected.

"Are you okay?

"Do I look okay?"

Louise started to say something but changed her mind. Louise walked further into the room.

"What are you going to do about Ron?"

"I have decided to divorce him and let him have whoever he wants."

"Is that what you really want?"

"Right now I'm not sure of anything."

"Well, don't make any decisions until you're sure this is what you want."

"Did you hear how he took her side? Can you believe that?"

"Trina I know you don't want to hear this, but I am going to say this anyway. You took Ron for granted. Ron is a good man, he provided damn good for you and you took advantage of him. There have been many nights that I heard you guys arguing about sex. I don't understand how you expected your husband not to find comfort in another woman when you have made it so easy for him to do so. You plan to take a trip for two weeks and leave him behind with your young beautiful house guest and you expected nothing to happen. Are you stupid or were you so caught up in being with Martin that you didn't see this coming?"

"You're right, I don't want to hear this," Trina said as she walked into the bathroom.

"Well, you're going to hear this," Louise said as she followed Trina.

"What are your plans once you divorce Ron? Do you think Martin is going to provide for you? Martin is a handsome man and his sex may be good, but that's it, he can't provide for you financially or do you plan to go back to work? Have you thought about these things? Please don't make decisions without thinking the entire situation through, please because you will only hurt yourself?"

"Trust me, I know what I'm doing."

Ron and Tracy were heading to the store when Ron remembered something.

"Oh shoot, I need to run back to the house for something," Ron said.

As Ron ran inside to grab his wallet off the sink in the upstairs bathroom, he heard Louise and Trina talking. He heard Louise talking about Martin. His heart stopped or though it seemed that way. He always wondered about Trina and Martin, but now it had been confirmed. She had slept with Martin and from what he heard, she was still sleeping with him.

Ron walked into the room and the women could have fainted. He said nothing as he walked into the bathroom where Trina stood and grabbed his wallet.

"Ron can we talk."

"Talk, what is there to talk about? The next time you want to have a conversation about who you're fucking and it's not your husband make sure your husband is not around."

Trina's mouth dropped open.

"Ron please, we need to talk."

"There's nothing for us to talk about. You want a divorce, you got it. I'll have my attorney draw up the paperwork and believe me, you won't get shit."

"Ron please talk to her before you file, please."

"What is there to talk about Louise? She goes away and comes back accusing me of something when she's the one that's been cheating. And oh, by the way, Tracy is much better in bed than you will ever be."

"You go to hell and take that bitch with you."

"I've been in hell for the last twenty years and yes, she's already with me," Ron said as he walked out.

Trina was so angry that she cried. "I want to kill his ass and that bitch."

Louise was stunned. She had never seen Ron like this before. She guessed hearing about Martin and Trina was just too much for him. Louise was thankful that he walked out and did not slap the shit out of Trina like some men would have done.

CHAPTER TEN

When Ron got back to the car, Tracy could tell something was wrong. His demeanor was very different from earlier.

"Is everything okay?"

"I'm filing for a divorce."

"What happened?

"I don't want to talk about it right now," Ron said as he drove off.

Tracy wished she could have been on the inside when Ron went back in she could only imagine what happened.

"What do you have a taste for? Ron asked.

"Some fried chicken, potato salad, baked beans and chocolate cake."

Ron laughed.

"Oh, I see you're hungry."

"Very. Ron, can I ask you a personal question?"

"Sure, go ahead."

"Why didn't you and Trina have any kids?"

"Trina didn't want any kids. So I have been deprived again just to please her."

"That is so selfish. If I got pregnant how would you feel about it?"

"You think you're pregnant already?"

"No silly, I just wanted to know how you would feel."

"I would love to be a dad."

Tracy's heart jumped for joy. She was falling for Ron and wanted to have his kids. She wanted to please Ron in every way possible. Tracy felt that he deserved the best because he was the best. Tracy could not believe that Trina would rather waste her time on Martin a loser than to be with Ron. Oh well, that just left room for her to be with Ron.

Ron pulled into the grocery's parking lot. He cut the engine, took the key of out of the ignition, but before he got out, he looked over at Tracy.

"Tracy can I ask you a question and I want you to be honest. Do you see yourself marrying a man my age?"

"Ron you are not that old and the answer to your question, yes, I could see myself marrying a man your age if his name is Ron Patterson hell yeah."
Ron threw his head back and laughed.
"That's what I wanted to hear."

After they were finished grocery shopping, Ron drove to Sahm's Park. He found a quiet area where they could eat, talk and be comfortable.

"This tastes so good. I guess I was hungrier than I thought. Thank you so much, Ron, for siding with me. If you had teamed up with Trina against me, I don't know what I would have done."

"Don't worry about it. She set her own fate when she left me behind to go to LA to be with Martin."

"I still can't get over that. Martin is handsome and his dick is big, but you're even more handsome and your dick ain't bad at all."

"Aw, so his dick is bigger than mines?"

"Ron," Tracy said as she pushed him away.

"He's just a little bigger, but bigger is not always better."
Ron and Tracy sat talking and ate for hours. They really got to know more about each other. Tracy was so intrigued with Ron and how he became so successful.

"Ron I want to apologize to you. You are a married man and I caused you to commit adultery and for that, I am very sorry, but I couldn't help myself. I know that who we marry may not always be the one that God wanted us to be with so knowing that makes me feel a little better, but adultery is still adultery."

"You don't owe me an apology. I made love to you because I wanted to, not because you made me. I could have easily walked away trust me. You will not believe how many women have hit on me and I didn't budge. Trina's friend Gloria tried to hit on me, but I never told Trina and I ignored her advances."

"If she knew that she would have gone through the roof. She seems so selfish to me. Why did you stay with her all these years?"

"Because I don't believe in divorce unless someone in the relationship commits adultery. I guess I knew she was sleeping with Martin and I didn't want to face the fact, so I ignored my feelings because I knew she would never leave me for him, but when you came along and seduced me, I was awakened and wanted to live a different life than I had previously lived."

"Oh, I seduced you now. If I recall you're the one who chased me in the pool and took advantage of me."

"That's your word against mine," Ron said.

"Well, I think we should head back even though I don't want to. I am seeing my attorney tomorrow to get the divorce process started."

"Oh, so you are serious?"

"Did you think I was joking? I'm telling you now I don't know how Trina is going to act, so just watch out or would you feel better if I put you up in a hotel?"

"I think I would feel better in a hotel, but I want you there with me."

"Right now I have to stay at the house. It wouldn't look too good if I moved out or starting spending the night away that would be something she could use against me."

"I see, but I have to get my things from the house."

Once Ron and Tracy made it back to the house, Trina was waiting for their return. Tracy went straight to her room, got some of her belongings, and waited for Ron in the car. She wanted out of that house as quickly as possible. Any items she left, she would have Ron get them another time. Ron made his way to the kitchen to grab a bottle of juice.

"Did you and your little bitch have a good day today?" Trina asked.

"Yes, we had a lovely day, how about you?"

Trina was so mad she wanted to slap the shit out of Ron and his sarcastic ass.

"Just so you know I will be stopping by Jeff's tomorrow to start the divorce process and just know that you will not get this house. This house will be for my next wife and my kids." Ron said as he turned to leave.

Trina lost it. She threw a bottle at the back of Ron's head. Ron turned around, grabbed a hold of her and shook the shit out of her.

"Woman, have you lost your fucking mind?"

Louise ran to the kitchen when she heard the glass break.

"You two stop that nonsense and Ron get your hands off of her."

Then Louise saw the blood running down the back of his head and on his shirt.

"Trina, did you do that?"

"Yes, she's crazy as hell. I don't know what's gotten into her."

"Oh my God, Ron come here and sit down while I go grab a towel."

Louise stood behind Ron with the towel and applied pressure to the back of his head to trying to stop the bleeding.

Tracy sat in the car for as long as she could. She had a feeling something bad was going on so she made her way back inside and down the hall to the kitchen where she found Ron and Louise. Tracy moved further into the kitchen and then she saw the blood.

"Ron, what happened?"

"Trina's crazy ass hit me in the head with a bottle."

Tracy walked behind Ron to get a good look at the cut.

"Do you think he needs stitches?"

"It looks pretty deep," Louise said.

"Ron I think you should go to the hospital to get this looked at."

"I have to agree with her Ron," Louise said.

Ron was hurt to his soul. He had never done anything wrong to Trina until he slept with Tracy, but Trina cheated on him long before this. He treated Trina like a queen and this is how she treated him. This was definitely the last straw that held their marriage together.

Ron and Tracy checked into a hotel around 3 am after getting back from the emergency room. Ron had to get six stitches. Tracy talked him into staying because she didn't know what would happen if he went back home.

Tracy was a little worried about Ron because he tossed and turn the entire time and he was constantly moaning. She woke him up to take some pain medicine because he continued to moan and once the medicine kicked in he slept peacefully.

Tracy let Ron sleep in since it took him forever to start sleeping comfortably. At 10:30, she called room service and ordered breakfast for them. She continued to let him sleep until the food was delivered. When she finally woke him up, she had everything set up so nice and neat. She catered to his every need. She fed in bed and later sexed him down real good.

"Damn, I could get used to this treatment."

"I just bet you could."

"So what time are you going to see your attorney?"

"Let me check to see if he can fit me in. Can you hand me my phone babe?"

Ron was on the phone with his attorney. Jeff told him that Trina has already called him.

"You got to be kidding me. Did she tell you that she busted me in the back of my head with a bottle and I had to get six stitches?"

"I didn't think so. Did she tell you she's been sleeping with Martin? See she didn't tell you any of that. Okay, I will be there shortly."

After Ron got off the phone, he turned to face Tracy. "I can't believe Trina. She called Jeff trying to tell him that I slept with you right under her nose and all this other bullshit and she hasn't said anything about any of the bullshit she has done. Well, at least I have proof that she busted me in my head. I could have her ass arrested if I wanted to."

"I know she's your wife, but if she lays a hand on you again, I will forget about her being your wife and beat that ass."

"Aw, you're going to take up for daddy," Ron said as he pulled Tracy onto his lap.

"You got that right daddy." She said as she kissed his lips.

Before heading to see his attorney, Ron had to stop by the house to get a few items and a change of clothes. He half expected to have another run in with Trina. This time he would be ready, but to his surprise, she was nice to him she even apologized for hitting him.

"Ron, baby can we try to work things out?"

"You should have thought about that before you slept with Martin."

"I'm sorry Ron, but Martin doesn't mean anything to me you do."

"You know you have a funny way of showing me how much I mean to you. You cheat on me, deprive me of having kids and then you hit me in the back of my head with a bottle. Is that how you show someone that you care about them? I think not. You just realized now what's at stake when I divorce your ass. It's too little, too late to try and pretend to care."

Ron left her standing in the hallway looking stupid.

Later that evening when Ron made it home, he walked upstairs to their bedroom to find Trina, but she met him at the top of the stairs. He pulled some paper out of his jacket and handed it to her.

"You have 60 days to find another place to live. Maybe Martin can help you and before you leave, I will need the keys to the beach house."

"You really did it. Ron, what can I do to change your mind?"

"Trina I can put up with a lot, but when you try to hurt me physically, I cannot tolerate that. I have never laid one hand on you no matter how mad you have made me and then to top that, you had the nerve to call Jeff and try to make me look like the bad person when you know I have been nothing but a good husband that tolerated all of your bullshit. No more babe, stick a fucking fork in me because I am done."

After gathering Tracy's items out of the room, he put them in the trunk of his car and went back inside the home.

"Oh, you might want to sleep in the guest room tonight because I am sleeping in our bedroom."

"So now I can't even sleep in my bedroom?"

"You can, but I wanted you to know that I was sleeping there."

Ron walked outside to call and check on Tracy.

"I'm home and everything is okay."

"Ron I want you here with me."

"I know I want to be with you as well. Just 60 days and everything should be final. I was just calling to say good night and if you need anything, don't hesitate to call me."

"Okay. Good night Ron."

CHAPTER ELEVEN

Ron took a shower and was in bed early. He didn't sleep well the night before because of the pain from his head, but tonight he took his pain pills and was knocked out in no time.

Trina stayed downstairs in the kitchen for hours trying to come up with a way to win Ron's heart back. Trina looked at the clock on the microwave and decided to head up upstairs to bed. She climbed the stairs slowly as she anticipated the reaction she would get from Ron.

She opened the door to the bedroom half expecting it to be locked, but to her surprise, it was unlocked. Trina walked in and closed the door behind her. Trina moved further into the room, walked over to Ron's side of the bed and watched as he slept. Minutes later, she walked over to the other side of the bed, dropped her robe to the ground exposing her naked body and crawled in bed with Ron. Trina pulled the covers off of Ron and slowly pulled his boxers down. She then crawled between his legs and began to flick the head of his penis with her tongue while gripping the base of his penis with her hand moving it up and down until it became long and hard. Then she took him in her mouth and seconds later, Ron began to stir in his sleep.

"Oh, Tracy baby this feels so good."

Trina stopped, she thought she heard him call her Tracy, but continued to suck his penis when she heard him loud and clear this time.

"Damn Tracy, oh baby, I love it when you do this."

When Trina heard this, she bit down on his dick as hard as she could.

"Tracy, what the hell are you doing?" Ron yelled out in pain as he grabbed his penis, reached for the lights and saw Trina instead of Tracy.

"Wrong, bitch!" Trina said as she grabbed her robe off the ground and walked out of the room slamming the door behind her.

"You are fucking crazy!" Ron yelled out to Trina.

Ron made his way to the bathroom to see the damage. He could tell that she broke the skin of his penis but was afraid he was bleeding. As soon as he flicked the light switch on, he saw the blood.

"Oh my God, I'm not even safe in my own home anymore."

Ron grabbed some bandages to stop the bleeding. Once the bleeding stopped, he applied some ointment to the affected area and wrapped it.

Ron made his way back into the bedroom, walked over to the door and locked it. He even put a chair up against the door.

Trina decided to sleep in the bedroom downstairs. She was furious and hurt that the man she had been married to for over 20 years, called out another woman's name while she was trying to please him orally.

The next morning Ron awoke early, his penis area was sore as hell, but he refused to let that get in his way. He had several things that he needed to do today like visiting his attorney. He wanted Trina out of the house immediately and he wanted to see Tracy. Ron was so glad that Tracy decided to stay in a hotel because there was no telling what Trina would have tried to do to her.

Ron shower and dressed in no time. He was serious. His attorney would have to do whatever he had to do to get Trina out of the house ASAP. He doesn't trust living with her anymore. What would she try to do to him next time, cut his penis off?

Ron walked downstairs to the kitchen before heading out and found Louise sitting there staring into space.

"Good morning Louise. Is everything all right?"

"Good morning Ron, but I think I should be the one asking if you're all right."

"I take it you heard us last night?"

"Yes. What in the world do you do to her?"

"What did I do to her, not a damn thing? She tried to bite my private off."

Louise laughed.

"I'm serious. I am going to go see my attorney this morning. I want her out of this house immediately. I don't trust being around her anymore. You know you are welcome to stay on with me or you can choose to go with her, it's up to you."

"Oh, I can't believe she did that to you. What has gotten into that woman?'

"Your guess is as good as mine, but I will not wait around to figure it out. Maybe Martin can help her figure out what's going on inside of that brain of hers."

"I'm heading out and I probably won't be back until this evening. If you need me, call me on my cell," Ron said as he kissed Louise on her forehead.

Ron called his attorney while he was on his way to see him. "I'm telling you I don't feel safe around her who knows what she will try to do to me next time. I want her ass out!" Ron yelled.

"Whatever you do, don't lay a hand on her." The attorney told Ron.

"I will not continue to let her hurt me. I will do whatever I have to do to protect myself and if that means knocking the fuck out of her, then that's what I will do."

"Let me see what I can do. It shouldn't be too hard since there's been violence on her part, but we can discuss things in greater depth once you get here."

Ron arrived at his attorney's office in no time.

"Hello, Mr. Patterson. Jeff's in his office waiting on you".

"Thanks, Rita.

Ron walked into Jeff's office.

"Thanks, Jeff for seeing me on such short notice."

"I'm just doing my job and being a good friend. Now let me see the back of your head. You said you had to get six stitches?"

Ron turned around so that Jeff could see.

"Yeah, I had to get six stitches."

"Damn, what did you do to her?"

"I said something she didn't like, but when she bit me, I was asleep."

"You're kidding me?"

"No, I had to lock the bedroom door last night and pulled a chair up to the door just to make sure she didn't come back to do me more harm."

"Oh no, she's got to go."

"I've been talking with my partners and they said I can have the court exercise equitable jurisdiction and order her to leave. I need you to explain to me in writing what she has done to you so I can take this to the judge. I have a meeting with him in an hour, so I should have some good news for you this afternoon."

"Okay, here you go I summed it up in one paragraph. I also have the hospital papers. I can take a picture of my dick if you think that would help."

Jeff laughed.

"Oh no, I don't think the judge wants to see that." Jeff shook his head.

"Well, let me get out of your here and I will wait for your call."

As soon as Ron gets to his car, he calls Tracy.

"Good morning sweetheart. How are you?"

"Good morning babe. I'm great now that I hear your voice. How are you?"

"I will be wonderful once I hear back from my attorney."

"Why, what's going on?"

"Last night while I was asleep, Trina tried to give me some head and I yelled out your name and she bit the shit out of my dick."

"Oh my, that bitch is really crazy. Ron, you need to stay with me until your divorce is final."

"Well, I am waiting for my attorney to get back with me. He's seeing the judge this morning about getting Trina out of the house today."

"That's good."

"Would you like to go to breakfast with me?"

"I would love to."

"Good I will be there in about fifteen minutes."

"Okay, I will see you then."

Back at the house, Louise sat Trina down and had a long hard conversation with her about her behavior.

"I know it's hurting you that your marriage is going down the drain, but doing what you have done to Ron will not make it any better. You are pushing him further away Trina. Besides, you're the one who started all this mess in the first place by having an affair with Martin. Trina, I am very disappointed in your behavior. You and I both know that Ron doesn't deserve you treating him this way. That man has done nothing but treat you like a queen and now you have gone and fucked that up. Just for the record, I will stay here and continue to work for Ron. I'm sorry Trina, but I have to think about what's best for me and being with you and Martin is not in my best interest if Martin will even be around."

Trina broke down and cried like a baby.

"I don't know what's gotten into me. I do love Ron no matter what anyone thinks or what I have done to him. I love him with all my heart. I just took him for granted because I thought he would always be there for me. I have to make things right with us."

"Honey, I'm not sure you can do that now. Maybe if you hadn't bitten him last night, but I know he's done. He went to see his attorney this morning to try to get you out of the house today. He doesn't feel safe around you anymore, so if I were you, I would start packing my belongings.

"Are you serious?"

"Yes, you have hurt him real bad and I doubt if he can ever forgive you for what you've done to him."

"Where am I going to go?"

"You can always stay at one of the rentals. I'm pretty sure he will let you stay there. He's not a mean or hateful person so I am sure he will not kick you out on the street and if you were smart, you would have been putting up money in your stash for something like this."

"Well, that I did. I guess I could purchase some rental properties and rent them out to keep some income coming in and that way I won't have to work a 9 to 5. I could also start my own business that I wanted to do a long time ago."

"Well, it seems like you will do just fine. Whatever you do, don't let that Martin talk you out of your money."

"Oh, I won't. I just can't believe this has happened. I would never have thought I would be divorced from Ron. I really love him. I can't just give him up without a fight." Trina began to cry again.

"I don't know how I can go on living without him."

"Don't start talking like that. You are strong you will make it. It will hurt for a while, but each day will get better just know that."

"That's easy for you to say because you're not getting a divorce."

"Honey I have been divorced twice cheated on both times so I know what you're going through, but the thing is, I never cheated on either one of my husbands."

Just then, the doorbell rang. When Louise opened the door, she came face to face with a sheriff's deputy she knew exactly what that meant.

"Is there a Trina Patterson here?"

"Yes hold on for just one minute."

Louise walked back into the kitchen to get Trina.

"There's a deputy out front that wants to speak to you."

Trina went to the door with a puzzled look on her face.

"Are you Trina Patterson?"

"Yes, I am."

The deputy hands her a document."

"You have been served."

Trina snatched the document from his hand.

"Thank you very much!" She yelled as the deputy walked away.

Trina slammed the front door and made her way back to the kitchen. Once she was in the kitchen with Louise, she read the notice out loud.

"I can't believe the court is making me leave. I have 48 hours to evacuate the premises. This is some bullshit."

Back at the hotel, Ron and Tracy relaxed after breakfast and was watching a movie when Ron's phone rang.

"Hey, Jeff, what's up?"

"I just wanted you to know that the sheriff's deputy served Trina with the evacuation papers, she has 48 hours to leave the premises. I suggest you stay somewhere else until then."

"But what if she destroys the house? I have to be there to make sure she doesn't leave with anything, but her belongings."

"I don't advise you to do that, but that's on you."

"Okay, thanks Jeff for everything."

"Well, she's been served with the evacuation papers?" Ron said to Tracy.

"That's good to know. How much time are they giving her to leave?"

"She has 48 hours to leave.

Forty-eight hours later, Trina moved into a four-bedroom tri-level one of their rental properties. She called Gloria and Renee to come over and help her decorate her new home. She was excited at times and sad other times because she never thought her marriage to Ron would ever end. Trina still had hopes of rekindling things with Ron, but as each day went by, she had less and less hope of that happening since Tracy was still in the picture.

Martin and Trina started seeing each other on a regular basis. She was planning to have a house warming party where she would let the world know that she and Martin were together since Ron moved Tracy in with him. Trina felt there was no need to keep Martin a secret anymore since Ron already knew about their affair.

The day of the housewarming party had Trina so stressed out,she wanted everything to be perfect.

"I can't believe Gloria is not here yet," Trina said to Renee.

"You know she's been acting a little weird lately. I wonder what's going on with her." Renee replied.

"She's supposed to pick up the cake for me. The place closes in ten minutes. I hope she makes it before it closes."

"I don't know. Why don't you call the store and see if she's been there so you can stop worrying."

"Great idea."

Trina called the store and got no answer.

"Shoot, they are already closed."

It was five o'clock and some of Trina's friends had started to arrive. Trina and Renee were in the kitchen having a glass of wine. There was still no word on Gloria.

"I am so through with Gloria. If she didn't want to do this, she should have told me I could have picked the cake up myself."

"Or I could have done it," Renee said.

Just then, Gloria walked in with the cake in hand.

"I'm sorry guys I'm late. I had so much to do today."

"I'm just glad you made it with the cake. For a while, I thought you were not going to show up." Trina said.

"I would never do you like that."

"I have a big announcement to make later, so make sure you two stick around."

"You need to tell us now. We're your best friends so we should know what's going on before anyone else". Gloria said.

"I agree." Renee chimed in.

"Nice try ladies but it's not going to happen. You will find out when everyone else finds out."

"Let's go, Ladies, help me carry the food out to the dining area," Louise said.

"Louise, thank you so much for agreeing to help."

"Trina just so you know, I will always be here for you no matter what. Just because I work for Ron doesn't mean our friendship has to end."

By 6 o'clock, the house was full of people, laughter, and food. Martin watched from a distance until Trina was ready to make her announcement. He stayed away from Gloria and only hoped and prayed that she would not be mad once the announcement was made and try to ruin things for him and Trina.

"Everyone can I have your attention, please! I have an announcement that I want to make."
Martin made his way to the family room to stand next to Trina. Gloria was excited to see him since she had not seen him since their time in LA, but she was also a little confused as to why he was there and standing right next to Trina.

"What's going on?" Gloria asked Renee.

"I guess we're about to find out now."

"As you guys know things with Ron and I are over. He's moved on with his life with someone else and so have I. I wanted to be the first to let you know so there will be no room for speculations. I am seeing someone as well. His name is Martin Jackson." Trina introduces Martin to her friends.
Gloria was stunned. She couldn't believe what she just heard.

"How dare that son of a bitch do this to me? He was fucking Trina the entire time he was fucking me. Well, wait until she finds out. Let's see if she still wants his whoring ass then."
Gloria walked up to where Trina and Martin were standing.

"Trina sweetheart, can I speak to you in private for a minute?"

"No Gloria Trina has guests to entertain. You can speak with her in private another time." Martin said as he guided

Trina away from Gloria. He knew what Gloria was trying to do.

"Not today, Gloria," Martin whispered in her ear before escorting Trina away.

Renee saw the interactions between Gloria and Martin.

"What was that all about?"

"What are you talking about?"

"You know damn well what I'm talking about. What did he whisper in your ear?"

"Renee mind your own fucking business."

"Trina is my business so again I ask you what he whispered in your ear."

"I'm outta here," Gloria said.

Later that night, Renee stayed so she could help Trina and Louise clean up.

"Trina when you have the time, I need to speak with you in private."

"Sure, let's step out onto the deck."

Trina and Renee made their way out onto the deck. "So what's up?"

"I hope I'm wrong, but I think something is going on between Martin and Gloria."

"What! Why do you say that?"

"Didn't you see Martin whispering something in her ear right after you made your announcement? She left right after that she was very upset."

"I did see that, but I thought nothing of it. I will ask Martin about later tonight."

CHAPTER TWELVE

"**Ron** I'm not feeling well. I think I should stay home today."

"Okay, sweetheart, do you need anything before I leave?"

"No, I just want to sleep."

"You've been sleeping a lot lately. Is everything okay?"

"Well, I didn't want to say anything right now, but I think I might be pregnant."

"What! Are you serious?"

"I took a pregnancy test and it showed positive. I need to make a doctor's appointment just to be sure."

"Oh my God, that's the best news that I have heard in months."

"Don't get too excited I want the doctor to confirm it first."

"Let me know when you have your doctor's appointment so I can go with you."

Ron stood up and started dancing and singing, "I'm going to be a daddy, I'm going to be a daddy."

"Ron stop it!" Tracy said laughing. "Get to work before you miss your Monday morning department meeting."

Ron sat on the side of the bed and pulled Tracy to him. "Knowing that you might be carrying my baby makes me the happiest man alive. I love you, Tracy Simmons."

"I love you too Ron Patterson," Tracy said as she allowed Ron's tongue to enter her mouth. "Oh Ron baby, I want you so bad."

"Tell you what. Once my meeting is over, I will come back and work from home. Then you can have as much of me as you like."

Trina sat parked down the street and waited for Ron to leave for work. She already knew Ron had moved Tracy into her house and she wanted to let Tracy know that she held no hard feeling toward her.

Tracy was trying to go back to sleep when she heard the doorbell ringing and then she heard voices. She recognized Louise's voice, but she could barely hear the other female's voice, but she could tell it was a female.

"I come in peace Louise. I just wanted to see how you were doing since I haven't heard from you since my party and I wanted to drop off some things for Ron and Tracy."

"Oh, how sweet," Louise said.

"I know how much Ron loves his coffee and his vitamin water. I figured Tracy could help him drink some of it. I was at the store and I automatically thought of Ron. I hope Tracy doesn't mind."

"I'm sure she won't."

Tracy walked downstairs to where she heard the voices. She was shocked to see Trina standing in the kitchen.

Louise turned to look when Tracy walked in.

"Good morning Tracy," Louise said.

Trina turned to face Tracy.

"Good morning Tracy," Trina said.

"Good morning ladies," Tracy replied. She was shocked at Trina's kindness.

"I was telling Louise that I brought over some things for you and Ron. I hope you don't mind."

Tracy peeked inside the grocery bag and wondered why she would buy things for her and Ron. "What is she up to?" Tracy wondered.

"Oh, I see," Tracy said as she looked at Louise with a puzzled look on her face.

"That was nice of you Trina, but if you two would excuse me, I am going to go back to bed. I'm not feeling well today."

"Did you eat too much this weekend at the barbecue? I heard you and Ron hosted our annual barbecue feast that we used to do every year." Trina said.

"No, I think I might be pregnant," Tracy said, trying to piss Trina off.

Trina's heart dropped to her stomach, "Oh, you fucking little whore!" The words left Trina's mouth before she realized it.

"What! I got your whore. You need to leave now. Louise can you make sure she leaves and that she doesn't step foot in this house ever again." Tracy said as she headed upstairs.

"Trina why don't you stop with all the bullshit," Louise said as she escorted Trina to the front door.

"Louise, please make sure Ron gets my gifts."

"All right, I will Trina."

Trina was in tears when she left. "That's okay you two motherfuckers will get yours." She said as she got in her car.

When Trina made it back home Martin was waiting on her.

"Where have you been this early?"

"I went to the grocery store."

"Well, what did you get?"

"I got some stuff for Ron and Tracy," Trina whispered as she moved past Martin.

"You what, did I hear you correctly? You said you bought Ron and Tracy some stuff at the grocery store?"

Trina ignored Martin's question.

"Trina, answer my question." He said as he grabbed a hold of her arm.

"Martin I don't have time for the bullshit. I bought Ron and Tracy some coffee and vitamin water. Trust me, you don't want to know any more than that. While you're here, what's going on with you and Gloria? What did you whisper in her ear at my party right in front of my face?"

Martin looked stunned. "What are you talking about?"

"You know damn well what I'm talking about. Are you still sleeping with her? I'm giving you an opportunity to tell me the truth. If I found out later that you are, it's your ass."

"No, I am not sleeping with her anymore, I promise. You're the only one getting this pipe. I have a question for you, though. Are you trying to get back with Ron?"

"Do I look like I'm trying to get back with Ron?"

"You tell me. You're the one grocery shopping for him."

"Well, there's a reason behind that, trust me. Remember what we talked about the other night about the life insurance policy. He made a promise that he would not remove my name as the sole beneficiary."

"I hope you know what you're doing."

"Well, it was your idea. I did exactly what you said."

"I didn't mean for you to make it that obvious."

"Trust me they will never think about it."

Just as Ron promised, he was home after his morning meeting. Ron walked upstairs to their bedroom to find Tracy still asleep. He bent over and kissed her softly on her cheek. Ron tried not to wake her so he changed clothes in the bathroom. Just as he finished, Tracy collided with him in the bathroom. Unable to make it to the toilet, she vomited in the bathroom sink.

"I'm sorry." She said as she hung her head over the sink letting the water run.

"Aw, don't worry about it. Go back to bed and I will have Louise clean this up."

"I can't keep anything down, but I so hungry."

"How about I fix you some chicken noodle soup if nothing else you can drink the broth."

"Okay, can you bring me some water?"

"Sure thing, anything for my babies."

"Ron stop it."

"Oh, by the way, Trina stopped by this morning and dropped off some things she picked up at the grocery store for you and me."

"What! You are kidding, right?"

"Nope, ask Louise. I made her leave after she called me a little fucking whore."

"I'm going to tell Louise that I don't want her in this house ever again.

Ron walked downstairs to Louise's room just as she was coming out.

"Hey, Ron, what are you doing home?"

"I came home early to be with Tracy since she's not feeling well. She told me that Trina was here earlier. I don't want her in my house anymore, do I make myself clear?"

"Yes, I understand. She left you and Tracy some items in that grocery bag on the counter."

"Tracy had a little accident in the bathroom in our room, can you clean it up for me?"

"Sure, no problem."

Ron made his way into the kitchen. He pulled out the items in the bag. He put the vitamin water in the refrigerator before taking one out. Ron opened a bottle of the vitamin water and drank it straight down. "Damn that was good. Ron then puts the coffee in the coffee container.

He made his way to the pantry and got a can of soup, opened it and poured it into a pan. Ron turned the stove on low as he poured the contents of the soup in the saucepan.

Fifteen minutes later, he headed upstairs with soup, orange juice, water and some crackers for Tracy.

"Hey babe, wake up, I have some food and juice for you."

Tracy stirred awake and sat up in the bed with the pillows propped up behind her.

"Um, the soup smells good."

"If you ask me, the soup smells better than it really tastes."

"I take it you're not much of a soup person."

"Naw, not really."

"I will be downstairs in the study working so if you need anything just holler."

"Okay, babe, thanks."

Later that evening, Trina and Renee made an unexpected visit to see Gloria.

"I know she's here because her car is in the garage," Renee said as she knocked a fourth time.

"Maybe she's having company and doesn't want to be bothered."

Just as the women were about to leave, Gloria opened the front door.

"Are you busy?" Trina asked.

"No, come on in. What are you guys doing here?"

"I wanted to talk with you about the other night at my party. I want to know what and why did Martin whisper in your ear and why you left abruptly without saying goodbye?"

"Girl I had a bad headache and I didn't want to bother you so I just left. You should ask Martin about what he said to me."

"I'm asking you. I am very much aware of the fact that you've been fucking him behind my back and believe me if I found out that it hasn't stopped, I will fuck you up. Do I make myself clear?"

"You have a lot of nerve coming to my house threatening me. You better tell your man to stop calling me and trying to get me in bed."

Trina pulled out her cell phone and dialed Martin's number.

"We will get to the bottom of this right now."

When the phone rang, Trina and Renee looked at Gloria. Then out of nowhere, Trina hauled off and slapped the shit out of Gloria.

"Martin bring your ass out here right now!" Trina yelled. By this time, Renee was standing in the middle of Gloria and Trina as Martin slowly walked in the living room with nothing on but his boxers.

"I'm sorry Trina. I tried to break it off with her, but she threatened to tell you if I did not come here this evening and baby I didn't want to lose you."

Martin said as he moved in to hug Trina.

"Don't you dare touch me, Martin! You didn't even have enough respect for me to put your clothes on before coming out."

Trina said as she grabbed her purse and walked to the front door.

"It's a shame that our friendship had to end because of your no good for nothing ass."

Renee followed behind Trina as the two made their way back to Trina's car.

"I can believe this shit."

"Well, it's better that you found out now rather than later."

Trina continued to drive as the tears ran down her face.

"I can't win for losing."

Renee grabbed a hold of her hand.

"I know it feels like that right now, but things will get better."

Later that night, Trina packed all of Martin's belongings, put them in one of the bedrooms downstairs, and headed upstairs to take a shower and go to bed.

Martin parked down the street and waited until he saw the lights go off downstairs before entering the house. He knew Trina was very upset with him about being at Gloria's today, but shit, he couldn't help it that these old cougars offer to pay him just to please them.

Martin eased the door open trying his best not to make any noise. He quickly walked up the stairs to the bedroom where he heard the shower running. He undressed quickly and headed for the shower to join Trina.

"Oh no, the fuck you don't," Trina said as she slapped Martin across the face. "Get the fuck out of my house now! Go and make someone else's pussy rain tonight boo."

Martin laughed.

"You're so funny and so pretty when you're angry." Martin walked up to her, slid his hand between her legs, and began to rub her clit. "Martin stop!"

"Do you really want me to stop?"

"Yes!" Trina said, but her face told him differently. Martin began sliding his two fingers in and out of her as she began to melt.

"Do you want me to stop?"

Trina breathing began to speed up. "Martin please," she said as she held him tightly.

"Trina I don't know if you want me to stop or continue. You have to tell me, baby? Tell me what you want."

"Martin I want you to fuck me and fuck me real good."

Martin picked Trina up and carried her to the bed where he laid her down and she spreads her legs for him. Martin buried his head between her legs and went to town. He then moved slowly up her body planting kisses everywhere until he reached her breast. He took one in his mouth and sucked on it until she cried out. Martin moved his penis up and down her pussy making her want him even more before entering her. Once she was there, he inserted his penis slowly inch by inch until he disappeared. He then grabbed her legs and placed them on his shoulders moving slowly in and out going deeper and deeper.

"Aw Martin baby this feels... oh, Martin shit!"
They both exploded at the same time. "Damn baby your pussy clamped down on me like a motherfucker. I thought for a minute you were going to squeeze all my shit out." They continued to lay there until they both passed out from exhaustion. The next morning, Martin made breakfast and had everything ready for her when she made it downstairs.

"Good morning babe," Martin said as he kissed Trina on the lips.

"Do you want coffee or orange juice?"

"Coffee's fine."

"I packed all of your shit. It's in the bedroom down the hall."

"Oh, so you want me out now?"

"What do you think?"

"Look, Trina, I promise you, it's over between Gloria and I. I don't want to lose you over her. You have to believe me. Baby, we are good together and our loving is off the chain."

"If you felt that way, then why did you continue to sleep with her?"

"I was just being greedy for the money. She was paying me $500.00 each time I would have sex with her."

"So you were prostituting yourself. How do I know that you're not doing this with anyone else or if you're telling me the truth about it being over with you and Gloria?'

"You don't you just have to trust me."

"Well, I don't believe you. I have no trust in you right now."

"I know I will have to earn your trust again, I understand that and I have no problem with that."

"Okay, we will see and if you fuck up, it's over and I mean it."

CHAPTER THIRTEEN

The next day Tracy went to the doctor and Ron accompanied her. They were in the examining room waiting on the results of the pregnancy test.

The doctor walked back into the room. Well, I have your results here. It shows that you should be about two weeks pregnant. Ron jumped for joy. "Are you serious?" The doctor laughed.

"Yes, I am very serious. I take it that this is your first one?"

"Yes, it is," Tracy said not believing what's happening right now.

She had gone from robbing Peter to pay Paul to living the good life like she always wanted and now she's going to have a baby. This can't get any better she thought.

Ron was so excited when they returned home.

"Louise," Ron yelled.

"What's wrong?" Louise asked as she came out of her room.

"We're having a baby!" Ron shouted.

Louise laughed with joy. She was truly happy for Ron.

"Well, congratulations you two," Louise said.

"When's the due date?"

"In about 8 ½ months," Tracy said.

"Well, we will have to take good care of you until then," Louise said.

I need to run out for a while. Tracy, do you need anything while I'm out?"

"No, I'm fine."

"Louise can you prepare something special for dinner, I have a surprise for you guys?"

"Yes, I can do that."

"I am going to lie down and get some rest if you two don't mind."

"No, go ahead babe and I will be back shortly," Ron said as he kissed her on the lips.

Ron turned to leave and all at once, he felt lightheaded and stumbled against the wall.

"Ron, are you okay?" Tracy said as she ran to him.

"Here come in the family room and have a seat for a minute," Louise suggested.

Ron laid his head back on the couch. "I don't know what happened. I felt like I was going to pass out."

"We can't have that. You need to make a doctor's appointment." Tracy said.

"Has this happened before?"

"No babe it hasn't."

"Ron you need to take care of yourself. I don't want to raise this baby without you."

"I know I want to be around just as much as you want me around. Just let me lie here for a few minutes, then I should be fine."

"Take all the time you need," Louise said. "Can I get you something to drink?"

"Yeah grab me one of those vitamin waters."

Tracy rolled her eyes.

"I'm sorry baby. Why let them go to waste?"

"She probably poisoned them."

Ron laughed. Trina is crazy, but she's not that crazy."

"Right."

After a few minutes, Ron felt better. He drank the vitamin water and headed out.

"I won't be long."

"Okay, Ron I will be upstairs."

Gloria was furious, she had been calling Martin ever since he left her place last night, but he never answered. He was supposed to be going to the drug store, but he never came back.

"Where the fuck is he?" Gloria said, pacing back and forth in her living room. "He better not be with that damn Trina I know that."

Martin checked his phone for the tenth time. "Damn, I wish she would stop calling me."

Martin decided to send Gloria a text message breaking it off with her.

"Gloria it is over between us. I am staying with Trina. Sorry and Good Bye!"

Gloria was sitting on the couch watching television when she received a text message from Martin. "Oh hell fucking naw, you're ending this with a text message. Well, we will just see about this."

After reading the message Gloria showered, dressed and was heading in Trina's direction. Ten minutes later, Gloria pulled into Trina's driveway. She cut the engine, got out and walked up the walkway swiftly.

Martin and Trina were having lunch when they heard the doorbell.

"I'll get it," Martin said.

When Martin answered the door, he got the surprise of his life.

"I knew you would be here," Gloria said as she pushed him out of the way and entered.

By this time, Trina heard Gloria's voice.

"Oh hell no."

Trina made her way to the foyer where Martin and Gloria stood arguing.

"Bitch you have a lot of nerve coming to my home. Get the fuck out of here while you still can." Trina said, pointing her finger and moving closer to Gloria. Martin stood in the middle of both women to make sure nothing happened. He knew both women were on fire because of him.

Trina and Gloria, please calm down.

"Why are you here?" Trina asked Gloria.

"Why don't you ask Martin?"

"Martin?"

"I told you I broke it off with her and that's why she's here."

Trina stood with both hands on her hips looking at Gloria.

"So why are you here?" Trina asked.

"Oh, so you told her you broke it off with me?"

"Yes, I keep no secrets from her," Martin said.

"And if you know like I know you will stop contacting him to fuck your old desperate ass."

"I'm neither old nor desperate."

"Please, anyone who pays a younger man to fuck them is desperate."

"Trina fuck you and Martin," Gloria said as she stormed out of the house.

"We will fuck each other, baby," Trina yelled out to Gloria.

"Why are you adding fuel to the fire?" Martin asked.

"Why do you even care?" Trina gazed at Martin.

"I'm not playing with you Martin it better be over."

"You heard what she just told you that I broke it off with her. What more do you want me to do?"

"I want you to do the right thing. I lost a lot to be with you just remember that."

That evening Ron, Tracy, and Louise sat down to dinner. Ron was all smiles.

"Tracy and Louise I just have to say right now I am the happiest man alive.."

"I have to say, Ron, I have never seen you this happy in a very long time and I know Tracy is the reason. I hate to say this, but at first, I didn't like or even trust you Tracy, but now you are all right with me just as long as you treat Ron right."

"Well, Louise you won't have to worry about that because I love this man with all my heart. I don't want to exist without him in my life."

Ron couldn't hold back any longer.

Ron stood, reached in his pants pocket, pulled out a box and bent down on one knee if front of Tracy.

"I know we have not known each other very long, but you bring something out in me. I love you and I want to spend the rest of my life with you and my baby that you're carrying, so with that being said, Tracy will you marry me."

Tracy was shocked since Ron and Trina's divorce wasn't even final. She hesitated at first but thought about it, fuck it, I love this man she thought to herself.

"Ron I love you very much and yes I will marry you." That night Ron and Tracy made love like no other time to celebrate their engagement.

Weeks and months went by and Ron continued to have those dizzy spells he even started vomiting every day. Tracy was so worried about him. They had been to two doctors and they couldn't find anything wrong with him. Tracy made him an appointment with a specialist. She was determined not to raise this baby by herself. She loved Ron more than anything and she did not want to exist without him.

When Trina found out about the engagement, she tried to put negativity in Louise's head. "Ron's getting sick every day, that bitch is probably trying to poison him and get all his money."

"Now Trina I don't believe that one bit," Louise said.

"Then what could it be? He wasn't sick when we were together."

"I'm not going to continue to have this conversation with you Trina. You and I both know that's not true. Why would she do this? She's three months pregnant and engaged to Ron?"

"You can think what you want to think, but I know different. Martin told me what type of person she really is and I wouldn't put anything past her."

"I think you should stop listening to the whorish ass Martin. Trina, I have to go, I will talk with you later." Louis hung up from Trina furious. That woman is losing her mind." She said to herself.

Just then, Ron and Tracy walked in from seeing the specialist.

"So how did it go?" Louise asked

"They ran some tests, but they won't know anything until the test results are back. They should be back within a week.

In the meantime, we have to write down everything he eats."
Tracy explained.

"I told him it's probably that damn juice and coffee Trina
brought over here," Tracy said.
Louise thought Tracy was playing, but she was serious.

"Hey babe, can I throw this shit away?" Tracy said,
pointing to the vitamin water and coffee."

"Naw babe that's not what's making me sick."

"Okay, if you say so. Why don't you go up and lie down
and I will bring you some food up."

"Make sure you bring me a bottle of that vitamin water."

"Right," Tracy said, rolling her eyes.
Tracy prepared Ron a ham and cheese sandwich with chips
and chicken noodle soup and some orange juice. She
deliberately left out the vitamin water. If he wanted that
bullshit, he would have to get that himself.

"Here you go, sweetheart. Would the baby like for me to
feed him?" Tracy said jokingly.

"I'm over here dying and you got jokes," Ron said
laughing.

"You better stop saying shit like that. If I lose you, Ron,
there is no reason for me to exist on this earth."

"What, you better be here to take care of my baby."

"Just eat Ron and get some rest and let's not talk about
not being here for each other."

Martin had been trying his best to earn Trina's trust
back, but it had been very hard especially with Renee in her
ear. If he didn't know any better, he would say she wanted
him to break her a piece off.
Every time he turned around, she was there. He didn't know
if he was fucking Trina or if Renee was or maybe they both
were.
Martin walked into the kitchen where he found Trina and
Renee.

"Damn you here bright and early," Martin said.

"Well, they say the early bird catches the worm," Renee
said.

"I don't eat worms so I wouldn't know anything about that," Martin said being sarcastic as he poured himself a cup of coffee.

"You're right, you're too busy eating other things," Renee replied as she smiled at Martin.

"You're just mad because I won't eat your shit."

"You guys are too much," Trina said.

Martin kept his eyes on Renee and mouthed, "You want me to eat you?"

Renee smiled the biggest smile while nodding her head.

Now Martin knows why Renee has been hanging around.

"Damn these old bitches." He said to himself.

"Hey, Trina I'll be out back working on the lawn if you need me," Martin said as he made his way outside. Renee was beginning to make him a little nervous. He was trying to keep his promise with Trina, but these women were making it hard for him.

Renee eyed Martin until he was out of sight.

"So Trina do you really believe it's over between him and Gloria?"

"Oh yeah, she got the message loud and clear yesterday."

"Hey, do you think Martin can plant some shrubs in my yard by the windows?"

"You will have to ask him. He's been so busy with his lawn care business."

"Can I go out and ask him?"

"Go ahead."

Renee was more than happy to go out and speak with Martin.

Renee walked to where Martin was working. She looked at his strong back and his nice ass and when he turned around, her eyes were glued to his abs and moved down south to his groin area.

"Martin, Trina told me to check with you to see if you have any time to plant some shrubs in my yard."

Martin looked up and by the way, Renee was smiling at him, she wanted him to do more than plant shrubs.

Martin laughed and slowly licked his lips.

"I'll have to check my schedule and get back with you?"

"Okay and let me know how much you will charge me?"

"Here we go again," Martin said as he wiped the sweat from his face.

Now he knows why his parent's marriage was ruined. His mother always told him he was just like his dad and that he couldn't keep his dick in his pants, but he was determined to make things work with Trina and leave all the other women alone.

CHAPTER FOURTEEN

Ron ate his lunch and walked down to get a bottle of the vitamin water.

"Man, this stuff is so good."

An hour later, he was in the bathroom vomiting.

"See I told you to leave that shit alone. You're so hard headed."

Tracy was so upset that she grabbed the rest of the vitamin water, put it in her car, and threw away the coffee.

"I'm running an errand if Ron asks for me tell him I will be right back," Tracy said to Louise.

Tracy pulled into Trina's driveway, got out, grabbed the remaining of the vitamin water, and walked up the walkway. Martin, who was doing the lawn, noticed a car pulling into the driveway, and made his way inside, His mouth flew open when he opened the front door and saw Tracy. She looked damn good he thought.

Tracy was so focused on walking without dropping the box that she never noticed Martin standing in the doorway.

"Hello, Tracy," Martin said, causing Tracy to drop the box. She was in shock to hear the familiar voice.

"Hello, Martin." She said nervously. Feelings that she thought were gone came rushing at her full force.

Tracy stumbled back. Martin caught her just in time.

"Are you okay?" Martin asked, smiling from ear to ear.

"Yes, I'm fine. I just wanted to drop off this box to Trina." Tracy said loving the feel of being in his arms.

"What do we have here?"

"It's the items Trina brought over to the house for Ron and me, but I'm returning them."

"Oh, I'll make sure she gets them. You're looking really good Tracy."

"Thanks, Martin." Tracy couldn't even look at Martin. Tracy in no way wanted him to know that he affected her. Martin touched her hand and she thought she would melt.

"Come on inside."

Once she was inside and the door shut, Martin moved closer to her rubbing her stomach. "See this could have been ours."

"Martin, what are you talking about?"

"As I remembered you left me to handle things with Trina and Ron. How could you do me like that? I thought you loved me."

"I did and I still do."
Martin said as he slid his hand up Tracy's dress and under her panties.

"Aw pregnant pussy is so good I heard."

"Martin stop." Tracy tried to remove his hand, but the feeling took effect and she melted in his arms as he moved in to kiss her.

"Come on Tracy just let me stick the head in."

"No Martin I have to go," Tracy said nervously as she moved away from Martin and moved toward the door. Tracy opened the door and was out of there in no time. She made her way back to the car, but before she pulled off, Martin approached the car.

"Tracy I just wanted you to know that what we shared was real. You will always be here in my heart." Martin placed his hand over his heart.
Tracy pulled out of the driveway doing 90 it seemed like.

"OMG what the hell just happened." She said out loud. Tracy was so affected by seeing Martin that she had to pull the car over once she drove down the street. Then all at once, the tears began coming uncontrollably. She hadn't seen or heard from Martin since that horrible day. She had no idea how much he had meant to her until now.

"Oh God, girl, get yourself together."

After seeing Tracy, Martin started to second-guess his feelings for Trina. Could it be that his feelings for Trina were really the feelings that he had in his heart for Tracy? After Tracy pulled off, Martin sat on the steps trying to get his self together. The feelings that he had for Tracy were back and stronger than ever.

"I love and want you, Tracy Simmons no other woman will take your place," Martin said to himself.

Trina stood in the doorway and listened to Martin talks to himself.

"Who are you talking to Martin? And who was in this house?"

An hour later, Tracy pulled into the driveway, shut the engine and got out. She walked slowly to the house. Her thoughts were still on Martin. "Damn, he's gorgeous." She thought.

Tracy made her way to the door and was met by Louise.

" I'm so glad you're back. Ron is getting worse. I think we should take him to the hospital."

Tracy ran inside to find Ron on the bedroom floor almost unconscious.

"Louise call 911."

Ron was admitted to the hospital. Tracy and Louise sat out in the waiting area for hours before they knew anything. Then an hour later, the doctor came out to talk with them.

"We found traces of Dimethylmercury in his system. This deadly poison can be injected into food and juices. This colorless liquid is one of the strongest known neurotoxins. It's a good thing you got him here when you did, but he is not totally out of the woods."

"Oh my God. I told you it was that damn vitamin water from Trina." Tracy bent over and whispered to Louise.

Louise put her hand up to her mouth. "I hope not."

"Just wait until I get my hands on that bitch."

"Now Tracy you can't be sure."

"Martin," Tracy remembered. "I have to warn Martin not to drink it. Do you have Trina's number?"

Louise gave Tracy's Trina's number. Tracy walked outside the hospital to call Trina's phone, but unfortunately, no one answered.

"Shit!" Tracy made her way to the parking garage to get her car. "I guess I'll have to do this in person. God just give me the strength to face this beautiful man again." She said.

Tracy made it to Trina's in no time. She walked so fast she was at the front door in no time and to her surprise, Martin answered wearing nothing but a pair of shorts and a big smile.

"Oh Jesus, please."

"You back already?"

"I came to warn you not to drink the vitamin water that I returned to Trina. The bottles have been tampered with. I think Trina tried to poison Ron and myself."

"Oh, so you do care."

Tracy walked past Martin. "Where's Trina?"

"She's not here, but you're welcome to wait for her."

Tracy took a seat on the couch and Martin sat next to her.

"We can finish what we started until Trina gets here." Martin inched a little closer to Tracy and pushed her backward gently trying to be as careful as he could.

"I want you so bad Tracy." He said while trying to pull her panties down.

"Martin stop!"

"Do you really want me to stop?" Martin asked as he got her panties half way down, slid his two fingers up and down her pussy before pulling his dick out and entering her halfway.

"Oh, Martin." Tracy moaned.

Martin moved in and out slowly deeper and deeper. "Aw baby this feels so damn good. I love pregnant pussy.' He said between breaths.

Tracy tried hard not to get carried away by the feeling of Martin inside of her, but she missed being with Martin and most of all, she missed his sex.

Tracy jumped when she heard the sound of a car door shutting, but Martin continued to work his magic.

She had to push Martin off of her onto the floor. She stood up as quick as she could, pulled up her panties and made her way to the front door to meet Trina.

Martin sat on the floor in the family room until he got control of himself.

As Trina walked through the doors of her house, Tracy greeted her.

"Oh hell no, what are you doing here?"

"I came to warn Martin not to drink the vitamin water that I dropped off earlier. You know the shit you tried to poison Ron and me with. Just so you know Ron is in the hospital fighting for his life." Tracy said as she moved closer to Trina. By this time, Martin made his way to the foyer and tried to stand in the middle of the women.

"What's wrong with you?" Trina asked Martin who looked exhausted.

"Have you been fucking this bitch in my house?"

"Trina, don't go there," Martin said.

"You have haven't you?" Trina saw the look on Martin's face.

"I can't believe you."

"Trina if I were you I would be praying that nothing happens to Ron instead of worrying about who your man is fucking," Tracy yelled at Trina while pointing her finger in her face.

"I can't believe you. I catch you with my man in my home and then you try to accuse me of poisoning my husband. Yeah, he's still my husband bitch."

"Come on ladies, let's be nice about this."

"Tell that to the police when they come and question your ass. I wanted to warn Martin and now that I have done so, I am out of here."

"Good luck Martin."

Martin brought his two fingers up to his mouth and licked them.

"What the fuck was that for?" Trina said as she hit Martin in the arm.

Trina calm down. Is it true about the vitamin water?"

"What do you think? I did what you suggested."

"In no way did I tell you to poison them and you know that."

"Telling me to do and telling me how to, is the same thing."

"Bullshit! We talked about the easiest way to poison someone just in conversation. I had no idea you were asking about it because you wanted to poison Ron and Tracy. I'm a lover, not a murderer.

Tracy made it back to the hospital in no time. She had done her duty by warning Martin about Trina the rest is on him.

"Is there any news on Ron's condition?"

"No, he's still fighting."

"That's my baby daddy." She said as the tears began to roll down her face.

"I can't lose him, Louise, I just can't."

"You won't trust me, Ron's a fighter. If Ron won't fight for himself, he will fight for you and that baby."

"I hope so."

Later that evening the doctor came out to talk with Tracy and Louise.

"He's resting comfortably right now. There's nothing you guys can do so why don't you go home, get some rest, and come back in the morning and if his condition changes we will call you."

Tracy had fallen asleep when her cell rang. Thinking it was the hospital, she quickly answered on the first ring.

"Hey baby, did I wake you?"

"Who is this?"

"It's me baby, Martin."

"Martin, what do you want?"

"Aw, don't be like that. I miss you, Tracy. I miss eating that good pussy and riding you all night."

"Martin, who are you talking to?" Trina asked.

"I'll call you back," Martin said before hanging up and making his way back to bed.

"What are you talking about? I wasn't talking to anyone."

"You must think I 'm stupid."

Martin ignored Trina, got back in bed turned his back to her and went to sleep.

Little does Trina know Martin is growing tired of her. If she's not careful, this will be another man that she will lose.

The next morning Tracy and Louise were at the hospital early. Ron's condition improved a little, but he was still not out of the woods. The poison can take an effect several months after coming in contact with it.

Tracy was praying while holding Ron's hand when he opened his eyes and moved his hand.

"Hey, baby," Tracy said as she looked down at Ron.

"He's awake Louise."

Louise walked over to the other side of Ron's bed when his eyes started rolling back in his head and he went into convulsions.

"Oh my God! Get the doctor, Tracy," Louise yelled.

Tracy ran as fast as she could to the nurse's station.

The doctor and the nurses ran back to Ron's room and asked that Tracy and Louise step outside.

"Oh my God Louise, what is going on?" Tracy said as she let tears that she had been holding back fall.

Louise grabbed Tracy's hand and led her down the hall to the waiting area.

"Calm down Tracy and let the doctor and nurses do what they need to do. Everything will be okay." Louise only hoped and prayed that Ron would pull through, but right now, things didn't look so good.

An hour later, the doctor came out to talk with Tracy and Louise.

"We had to sedate him. Right now, he is resting so I suggest you guys go on home. We want to keep him sedated until he is out of the woods if that ever happens."

"What do you mean if that happens?"

"To be honest, things just don't like good for Ron right now."

Just then, Tracy looked down and placed her hand on her stomach. She had a bad feeling that she would end of raising this baby alone.

"We're going to be just fine sweetheart." She said as she rubbed her stomach softly.

"Can I see Ron before I leave?"

"Sure, go right ahead."

Tracy and Louise walked back to see Ron. Tracy bent down and kissed him on his lips.

"Ron the baby and I really need for you to get well. I can't make it without you. I don't want to exist anymore without you. You're my life, you're the air that I breathe without you, there's no me." Tracy said as the tears rolled down her face onto Ron's face.

Louise with tears in her eyes walked over and hugged Tracy as she grabbed a hold of Ron's hand and began praying.

"Father in the name of Jesus, I asked that you heal Ron's body like only you can do. Allow him to be a part of Tracy and the baby's life so that he can be happy for once. I ask that you give Tracy the strength to get through this not only for herself but also for the unborn child that is growing in her stomach. Father, I asked that you comfort Tracy and give her the strength and peace in her heart to survive. I know that your will, will be done and whatever your decision is, we will accept that. Father, I asked all these things in Jesus name. Amen."

CHAPTER FIFTEEN

Tracy made several trips to see Ron every day still his condition did not change. She knew who was responsible for Ron's current health condition she just had to find a way to prove it and that way was through Martin.

"Tracy I hope you know what you're doing because if Trina finds out what you are up to, there's no telling what she will do to either one of you."

"I know Louise I promise I will be careful, but I can't let her get away with this and if I'm wrong then I will apologize."

Tracy was ready to put her plan into action. She cannot afford to mess up, she had only one chance and that's it. Tracy left out and was on her way to meet Martin at a restaurant downtown. She only hoped he kept his word and did not tell Trina what was going on.

Fifteen minutes later, Tracy pulled into the restaurant parking lot. She scanned the parking lot to make sure she didn't see Trina's car anywhere. Something worried her about today's meeting. She didn't really trust Martin after all his lying, but he was her only hope of catching Trina and proving that she poisoned Ron.

Tracy walked into the restaurant she looked around the area until she spotted Martin sitting in the back in a booth. Tracy walked back to the booth removed her jacket and slid in on the other side of the booth.

"I hope you kept your word," Tracy said.

"Didn't I tell you I wouldn't tell Trina?" Martin replied.

"Yeah, but we all know your word ain't shit."

"Damn that was cold."

"It may be cold, but it's the truth and you and I know it."

"So what is it that you need from me?"

"Your sweet Trina poisoned Ron and I need to prove it. I want her ass behind bars."

"And how can I help you?"

"I need to get the vitamin water back that I dropped off last month or I need for you to get her to tell you that she injected poison into the vitamin water and coffee on tape."

"Why would I do that? What's in it for me?"

"Is that all you think about? Why don't you try to do something nice for someone that was damn good to you."

"And what if I can't get her to admit to it?"

"Then you can't, but at least try. Ron is in the hospital, he's not doing well and if he dies, then I want whoever is responsible for his death to pay."

"Why do you think Trina's behind it?"

"Why else would she buy us a container of coffee and a case of Vitamin water and as soon as Ron started drinking that shit he starts getting sick. Does it make sense for her to buy us anything, especially since he's divorcing her and having a baby with me? It just doesn't add up."
Tracy handed Martin a recorder.

"Here you can record your conversation with her on this. You owe this to me Martin for what you've done to me."

"The way I see it you came out on top behind my lying."
Tracy looked at Martin like really.

"So you think you did me a favor?"

"Pretty much."

"Do you think it's fair for me to raise my baby by myself and that my child will grow up without a dad because your girlfriend poisoned his or her dad?"

"No, I'm not saying that."

"Just get her to confess. That's all I am asking. You act as though I'm asking you to commit murder."

"So if Ron dies and Trina is convicted of his murder, what happens next?"

"What do you mean what happens next?"

"Where do we go from here?"

"Right now I can't think about that. Whatever happens, I will have to take one day at a time."

"Let me think about this and if I decide to do this, I will let you know tomorrow."

Tracy laid back against the booth and shook her head. She was furious with Martin. His only concern was if Trina was convicted what would happen to him.

"Shit you need to go to jail too." Tracy thought to herself.

"Okay Martin, do you promise to let me know tomorrow?"

"Yes, I will," Martin said as he rubbed Tracy's hand.

"I will be waiting for your call," Tracy said before getting up and heading for the door.

Martin continued to sit and think about what Tracy asked him to do. He knew Trina was behind Ron's sickness, but could he turn on her like Tracy wanted him to do. True, he would love to get back with Tracy if Ron passed away, but he could not guarantee Tracy would take him back, but he knew for sure if he didn't do this and Ron died, there was no way in hell Tracy would ever take him back.

Tracy sat in her car a few minutes before heading home. She wanted so bad to confront Trina and go to the police, but she knew she had to do this the right way and by getting her to admit to poisoning Ron would be all she needed.

Martin entered the home it was quiet and a little eerie. On the ride home, he thought about what Trina could do to him if she was capable of murdering someone. He knows he will have to be careful and not let her know that he is trying to trap her.

"Hey Trina, where are you?" Martin yelled as he peaked in the family room and then walked down the hall toward the kitchen.

Martin entered the kitchen, but Trina was nowhere in sight. He made his way upstairs to their bedroom where he found Trina sitting in bed staring at the wall.

"Hey, Babe what's wrong?" Martin asked as he sat on the side of the bed.

"Where were you, Martin?"

"I was out."

"I know that much stupid. Who were you meeting with?"

Martin's heart starting beating fast, "Oh shit she knows I was meeting with Tracy." He thought.

"You better not be fucking around with Gloria. I promise I will kill you both."

"Man, I haven't seen Gloria since that last incident. I told you I was through with her. You need to stop tripping."

"Yeah, I'm tripping all right."

Martin eased off the bed and made his way to the door. He was headed downstairs to the family room to watch television and to get his thoughts together. This was the second time that she threaten to kill him and Gloria if she caught them together. He wasn't worried about her catching them together because as he said he wasn't dealing with her anymore, but the thought of Trina threatening him had been too much. He began to think about how he would even start the conversation about Ron.

The next morning, Martin walked outside in the backyard to call Tracy.

"Hello."

"Hey Trac, it's Martin. I decided to help you."

"Great Martin, thank you so much, but I want you to be careful because there's no telling what she will do to you if she finds out you're trying to trap her."

"I know what she will do, she will kill me," Martin said as he turned to the sound of the sliding glass door opening. "Okay, I will put you on my schedule for next week. I will call you before I head your way. Okay, I will see you then."

"Who was that?" Trina asked as she walked up to Martin.

"That was a new client."

"Right."

"What, you don't believe me? Man give a brother a break."

"Yeah, I'm going to give you a break all right."

"All I know is if you keep on with the threats, I'm out of here." Martin looked directly at Trina. He was getting tired of her tactics.

Trina thought about what Martin said.

"I'm sorry baby, I just don't want to lose you," Trina reached out to hug Martin.

"If you keep it up, you will," Martin said as he moved to avoid Trina's hug.

Trina was shocked that Martin moved when she tried to hug him. She knew something was up with Martin she just couldn't put her finger on it.

"Okay, I see how you are," Trina said as she turned to leave.

Martin remained out back sitting on the deck relaxing and trying to come up with a way to approach Trina without her being suspicious. Lately, she's been very suspicious of him and in no way does he want her to think something is up with all the questions he will have to ask her.

"What do you want for dinner?" Trina yelled out to Martin who was still out back.

"I have a taste for pizza," At least she couldn't poison that he thought.

Trina joined Martin out back as they waited for the pizza.

"Oh, it feels so relaxing out here. I see why you come out here often."

"Yes, it is very peaceful and the breeze off the waterfall is not bad either. I could sleep out here if we had a tent set up."

"Would you really?"

"Sure wouldn't you?"

"No, I don't get into the outdoors like that."

"So if I bought a tent and had it set up and made it comfortable for you, you wouldn't sleep out here with me?"

"I don't know. That's something I would have to think about."

"After dinner, I want to go and buy a tent and some other things. I want you to sleep out here with me tonight. Deal?"

"I don't know we will have to see."

After dinner, Martin was true to his word. They went shopping for camping equipment and then they came home and put the tent together. He made the inside more of a room instead of a tent. This was his way of getting Trina comfortable. He would give her some good sex and wine before he began to question her. He had everything laid out he had the recorder on his side by his pillow he just hoped everything didn't go south.

Martin walked in the house to find Trina.

"Would you care to join me outside?"

"Aw, I don't know Martin."

"Just give it a try."

Martin guided Trina out to the tent. He unzipped the front of the tent and allowed Trina to enter.

"This is all for you sweetheart. I made sure you would be comfortable."

"Oh, Martin this is so nice. It doesn't even look like a tent inside."

"That was the point. I want you to sleep out here with me tonight."

"Don't give me that look," Martin said as he saw the look of apprehension on Trina's face.

"We will see."

"Have a seat and take your shoes off."

Martin hands Trina a glass of Red Moscato.

Trina sat down on the chair as Martin started to massage her feet as the sound of soft jazz echoed throughout the tent.

"Oh, this is so relaxing," Trina said as the sound of the waterfall right outside the tent mixed with jazz and the wine started to relax her mind.

Martin made sure the tape recorder was on and that there was enough tape to capture their entire conversation tonight.

"Did you know Ron was in the hospital fighting for his life?" Martin asked, trying not to sound suspicious.

"No, and how did you find this out?" Trina looked at Martin suspiciously.

"I overheard some people talking about it at the drugstore." He lied not wanting her to know that he met with Tracy yesterday.

"That's odd that you would run into someone who knows Ron at the drugstore."

"Did you mean it when you said you put something in the Vitamin water?"

"What! I never told you that. Why are you asking me about that anyway? Who put you up to asking me this?" Trina clearly became paranoid.

"What are you talking about? Calm the fuck down. No one put me up to do anything."

"That's it, I'm outta here," Trina said as she grabbed her shoes and walked back in the house.

"Damn, I did all this shit for nothing."

The next morning, Martin awakened to the sound of birds chirping and the sound of a lawnmower. He looked around at his surroundings until he realized where he was. Martin unzipped the tent, got out and stretched before heading inside. Once inside, he found Trina in the kitchen making breakfast.

"Good morning," Martin said.

"Good morning babe. I wanted to apologize to you for last night. I don't know what's gotten into me."

Now Martin knows Trina has something to hide he just had to catch everything on tape.

"Oh, don't worry about it."

"Are you hungry?"

"Yes, I'm am."

Martin and Trina sat at the kitchen table eating breakfast without saying a word. Martin's mind was busy trying to find a way to trick her into saying she poisoned Ron while Trina was wondering if she could really trust Martin anymore. At one time, they both talked about getting Ron out of the way, but she thinks Martin was just pulling her leg while she was serious.

Tracy was at the hospital with Ron when he awoke. He seemed to be doing a little better, but the doctor was still concerned. With this type of poison, it could take months for it to kill a person. He wouldn't be totally out of the woods until about six or seven months from now.

Ron was alert to Tracy, the doctor and the nurses. He was able to move his limbs, which was a good sign. His speech was normal as well.

"Oh baby, I am so glad to see that you're awake," Tracy said as Ron rubbed her stomach.

"How are you feeling?"

"I feel so weak. I'm so thirsty."

Tracy asked the nurse for some water for Ron.

"How's my baby doing?"

"Your daughter is doing fine."

"It's a girl," Ron said as he smiled.

"I was thinking about names for her. What do you think about the name Ronisha or Ronita?"

"That's good. I like Ronisha and Ronita. Either one would be okay with me."

"Can I get out of the bed?" Ron asked.

"I don't think you're strong enough to get out of bed, but I will ask the nurse."

Tracy walked back in the room with a nurse.

"So you want to try to get out of bed, I hear."

The nurses came in to help Ron get out of bed, but when he tried to stand, he got light-headed and had to sit back down.

"Maybe we can try again tomorrow."

"Okay," Ron said as he lay back down. "I guess I am not strong enough yet."

"You have plenty of time to gain your strength back so you can get out of bed and out of this place."

Each day, Ron got better and better and before he knew it, he was being released from the hospital, but not before one of the detectives came and had a conversation with him and Tracy about his situation.

After talking with Ron, the detective asked Tracy if he could speak with her outside in the hall.

"I know Ron doesn't think Trina has anything to do with this, but you do and it is clear that someone tried to kill him."

Tracy and the detective stayed in the hall for at least twenty minutes talking. Tracy agreed to meet with him one day next week at his office.

She and Louise were so glad to have Ron back home doing well moving around as normal.

Louise had notified Ron's Brother Kurt, who was out of the country about Ron condition. He wanted to come right away, but Louise told him she would call him if that was necessary.

Sitting outside the home for hours, she finally saw Ron as he walked outside to get his paper.

"That's a hard motherfucker to kill, but next time you won't be so lucky." She said as she parked two houses down.

Trina made her way back home, but what she didn't know was that Martin had bugged her car and he got her on tape. Trina pulled into the driveway, cut the engine and rushed inside.

"I thought you said Ron was on his death bed?"

"And how do you know he's not?

Trina rolled her eyes at Martin and headed upstairs to their bedroom. She still didn't trust Martin and each day she became more and more suspicious of him.

Once she was inside the room, she sat down on the bed. She had a bad feeling that something wasn't right, but she couldn't put her finger on it. Trina lay back on the bed and closed her eyes. Martin entered the bedroom and saw that Trina was sleeping so he ran out to her car to make sure the tape recorder was still in place before heading to the tent to listen to any conversation that transpired in the car.

CHAPTER SIXTEEN

Trina's eyes opened as soon as Martin left the room. Trina waited until she heard the front door shut before running into the spare bedroom to peek out the window to see what Martin was doing and wondering why he was inside her car.

"Why the hell is he looking around in my car and what is he looking for?" She asked out loud.

As Martin approached the house, Trina ran back to the bedroom and pretended to be asleep. Martin entered the house, walked back into the back, opened the sliding doors and headed for the tent.

Inside the tent, Martin turned on the recorder to see if any, conversations were recorded and just as Tracy thought, it was Trina all the time. Martin continued to listen until the conversation stopped. As he turned off the recorder, he heard some noise outside the tent, but by the time he got the tent unzipped, whoever it was had left.

Martin stepped out of the tent, looked around the backyard and glanced at the patio where the moving blinds caught his attention. He wondered if it was Trina outside the tent and if so if she heard the recording.

"Shit!"

The last thing Martin wanted was to let Trina know that he was on to her. He went back into the tent and made a call to Tracy.

"Hey, Tracy this is Martin. I have something you might want to hear. Meet me at the same place in about an hour."

"That was Martin, he's working with me and detective Stevens trying to find out if Trina is behind the poisoning," Tracy told Ron. "So whatever you do, you cannot tell Trina anything and do not let her in this house, no matter what." Tracy walked down to Louise's room. "Hey Louise, I just want to inform you that Trina is not allowed in this house or to deliver anything to Ron. You know Ron still has a soft spot for Trina and doesn't believe she's behind his poisoning."

"Huh, you don't have to worry about me letting her in here."

"I'm just checking to make sure we are all on the same page when it comes to Trina and this house."

Tracy walked back upstairs.

"I'm running out for a while do you need anything while I'm out?" Tracy asked Ron.

"Yeah, can you stop and get some orange juice and vanilla ice cream?"

"Sure, is there anything else you might need?"

"No that should be it."

Tracy kissed Ron on the lips, grabbed her purse and headed out to meet up with Martin.

Before pulling off, Tracy phoned the detective to let him know what was going on.

"Tracy be careful and call me as soon as you leave your meeting with Martin."

"Hey, Trina I am running out for a minute. I should be back within an hour or so." Martin yelled from downstairs to Trina upstairs.

Martin headed out and Trina rushed and grabbed her purse and car keys. She stood at the window waiting for Martin to pull out of the driveway so she could follow him in her car. As he pulled out of the driveway, he looked back at the window, he thought he saw a shadow move away from the window. He's a little paranoid right now because he senses Trina suspects something is going on with him.

Trina waited until Martin drove away from the house before hopping in her car. She sped down the street until she saw his car from a distance.

Martin continued to check his rearview window when he spotted Trina's car.

"I knew her ass wasn't sleeping."

Martin grabbed his phone and dialed Tracy's number, but he doesn't get an answer. "Damn." Martin pulled over and sent Tracy a text.

Trina is following me. Let's meet tomorrow same time and same place.

Martin pulled back onto the road and turned left at the first light going in the direction of the mall. Trina continued to follow behind him but kept her distance. She had no idea that Martin had already spotted her and changed plans. Martin continued to drive in circles confusing the hell out of Trina.

"What the hell is he doing making u- turns and shit?" Trina yelled.

Martin made a u-turn and another u-turn while Trina continued to follow behind him until she heard the sound of sirens behind her.

"I can't believe this."

Martin laughed as he sped off once the police car had stopped Trina. He dialed Tracy again and this time she answered. "Our meeting is still on. I'm heading in that direction as we speak."

Tracy had not checked her phone to see the message from Martin so she was already seated at the booth in the back of the restaurant.

After Martin pulled into the restaurant parking lot, he waited a few minutes before exiting just to make sure the coast was clear.

Tracy was on the phone when Martin walked up. He slid in the booth on the opposite side and touched her hand. He was still in love with Tracy and it hurt him that what they had ended the way it had.

"What's going on Martin?" Tracy asked.

"Trina is on to me. When I left out the house, she followed me until she was pulled over by the cops for making a U-turn following behind me."

Tracy laughed, "So you caused her to get a ticket."

"Yeah, she is going to be very upset with me, but it's her own damn fault for following me in the first place."

"So what do you have for me?"

"I got something I want you to listen to and let me know if this is what you need." Martin pushed play on the recorder.

That's a hard motherfucker to kill, but next time you won't be so lucky.

"Is that it?" Tracy asked.

"Yeah for right now."

"Um… I'm not sure that's going to be enough, but I will let the detective listen to it. I can take this with me, right?"

"Yeah, it's yours."

"Thanks, Martin, but I want you to be careful since Trina is so suspicious of you."

"Will you have dinner with me, Tracy?"

"Martin, I told you this would be strictly business."

"I know. I'm not trying to fuck you Tracy not saying that I wouldn't want to. I just want to have dinner with you, no strings attached. Is that okay?"

"Yeah, I guess that would be okay, but just dinner okay."

"Cool."

Martin waved the waiter over and she took their order.

"So Tracy how has life been treating you?"

"Do you need to ask Martin? You had me quit my job, give up my apartment and then you leave me to deal with Ron and Trina who threatened to call the cops on me because of your lies. Then I had to deal with the situation with Ron, who we thought we were going to lose while being pregnant. So how do you think life's treating me?"

"Tracy I am so sorry. I wanted you so bad that night at the club, and when you saw what type of car I was driving, I knew you were impressed. So when I asked you to go out with me the next day, I knew I had to continue to impress you. One lie turned into another lie and by that time, I couldn't turn back."

"Oh my God, I was so hurt behind your lies. I have never heard of such shit happening to anyone. I wanted to kill your ass."

"Trust me, I know I did you wrong and if I could go back and change things I would. I loved you Tracy and I still do. I would give anything if I could have another chance with you."

"Well, Martin you know that will never happen."

"Never say never Tracy you never know how life can change a person," Martin said as he waved his index back and forth.

Tracy rolled her eyes at Martin. "Trust me, honey, when I say it will never happen."

Martin was about to speak with the waiter showed up with their dinner.

"Saved by the bell," Martin said.

"Thank God," Tracy said laughing.

After dinner, Martin walked out with Tracy and walked her to her car. They were so busy talking that they never saw Trina pull into the parking lot. Trina pulled in, cut the engine, sat and watched the two until they both drove off.

"Oh, so it's like that now. You leave one bitch for another one.

By the time, Tracy made it home, detective Stevens was at the house. He could not wait to hear the conversation on the tape recorder.

Tracy pulled into the driveway, got out of the car and was greeted by the detective.

"Since I was already in the neighborhood, I figured I would stop by to listen to what's on the recorder."

"I don't know how much it will help, but come on in. Tracy, Ron, and detective Steven sat down at the kitchen table and listened to the tape. Detective Steven wiped his hand across his face and leaned back in the chair.

"I'm not sure this will help us out because it will be her word against ours as to who she was talking about and another thing, how do we know this is her? Does it sound like her?"

"It does and then it doesn't," Ron said.

Tracy looked at Ron, "how can you say that? You know that's Trina without a doubt."

"No Tracy I can't say one way or another. If I'm going to accuse someone of something, then I have to be sure. For all I know, you could be behind this. You got rid of the evidence. Why didn't you leave it if you were going to go and have Trina investigated."

"What! Are you crazy? Why would I want to poison you? What would I get out of it? It ain't like we're married and I would get all your money. I can't believe you right now."

Tracy got up from the table and marched upstairs to the bedroom. "I can't believe this shit," She said out loud. It seemed to Tracy that Ron had started to shy away from her ever since she started accusing Trina of trying to kill him. She can't believe he said she could have been the one that tried to kill him.

Tracy was so furious with Ron that she was on her way down to confront him when Louise stopped her.

"Come follow me."

Tracy followed Louise into her room.

"Is the door shut and make sure you lock it."

"What's going on Louise?"

"I hope I am wrong, but I think something's going on with Ron and Trina."

"What are you talking about?"

"Have a seat."

"Every time you leave the house, guess who Ron calls?"

"Who?"

"He calls Trina."

"So do you think they are trying to get back together?"

"Maybe."

"Louise I think you know more than what you're telling me."

"All I can say is put you some money away for a rainy day and don't put so much of your trust in Ron."

"You're scaring me, Louise. I'm carrying his baby."

"Was that the plan?"

"No, I didn't plan anything."

"I'm not talking about you. Just be careful sweetheart. You're a nice girl and I don't want to see you get hurt. Ron and Trina have been married for years. I've seen a lot of bullshit go on between the two, but they always seem to stay together. You know Trina always wanted a baby, she just couldn't seem to carry one to full term."

"Oh my God! Are you saying me getting pregnant was no accident and that Ron and Trina's plan was to get me pregnant?"

"I'm not saying anything, but who in their right mind would leave their husband behind with a beautiful young lady to travel with her girlfriends to another state? You tell me."

All kind of things started running through Tracy's mind. It was hard for her to take in what Louise was telling her.

"Thank you, Louise, for being honest with me. I thought Ron really loved me, but now, I'm starting to see otherwise." She said as she got up from the chair and made her way to the door.

Tracy walked to the front of the house to the family room. She stood for a moment before pacing back and forth trying to figure out what she was going to do. She was so confused and hurt that when her phone rang and she heard Martin's voice, she broke down.

"Tracy, what's going on babe?"

"Martin I need to see you." Tracy tried to say, but it didn't come out that clear.

"Meet me at our meeting place in ten minutes," Martin said.

Tracy tried her best to control her emotions, but she couldn't. As soon as she saw Martin, she broke down again.

"Baby, what is wrong?"

"I think they want my baby."

"Who wants your baby?"

"Ron and Trina. Louise said this in so many words. She told me to be careful. Louise said every time I leave the house Ron calls Trina. She also told me to put some money up for a rainy day. Martin, what am I going to do? Ron told me in front of the detective that it could have been me who tried to kill him can you believe that?"

Martin lay his head down on the table. He couldn't believe what was going on.

So what do you want to do? I don't think you should stay at the house anymore."

"Where am I going to go? I have nowhere else to go, plus I need to talk Ron into giving me some more money to add to my stash. I will move to the guest room and I will be very careful while I'm there. I have Louise looking out for me as well. I think she's starting to turn against them."

"Just be careful and don't worry about taking care of this baby by yourself, you will always have me," Martin said as he grabbed a hold of her hand.

"You should be very careful yourself. You're living with a bitch from hell and ain't no telling what she would do to you. You see how she busted Ron in the back of the head and tried to bite his dick off."

Martin laughed. "That was some funny shit right there. Ron is such a little bitch."

Martin and Tracy were in the middle of a conversation when Tracy's phone ranged.

"Hello."

"Hey, Tracy this is detective Stevens. I don't know what's going on with Ron, but he told me not to investigate this situation any longer. Do you think Ron and Trina are getting back together?"

"I don't know. Why do you ask that?"

"Well, things just seem to be different from before with Ron. He seemed to think you were behind all of it, but I don't buy that at all. When I left Ron's, I went over to speak with Trina and her voice matched the voice on the recorder. I want you to be real careful okay because something doesn't seem right with this situation."

"I will and thank you so much."

"That was the detective, he seems to think something is up as well. He went to talk to Trina and told me that her voice matched the voice on the recorder. He's not sure what the hell is going, but he told me to be careful. Damn, what am I going to do? I believe they want my baby. I will never let them have my baby."

CHAPTER SEVENTEEN

After the detective left, Trina got in her car drove around for hours trying to come up with a plan to get Martin's ass out of the picture and to get him back for being with Tracy. She was so angry with him. She wouldn't have been so mad if it had been Gloria, but since it was Tracy, she couldn't take it. "She has my husband and now my man." She said as she struck the steering with her fist. "I want my husband back now. Hurry up and have that damn baby so my husband and I can move on."

When Martin arrived home, he half expected to be greeted by Trina, but Trina was nowhere in sight. It was nighttime by the time Trina strolled in the house. She was tired, angry and confused. She couldn't understand why Martin would betray her.

Martin was asleep when Trina eased into bed. She was careful not to wake him. She lay in bed for hours thinking about things until she fell asleep.

The next morning, Martin rose early and was downstairs making breakfast when Trina walked in.

"Good morning," Trina said as she took a seat at the kitchen table.

"Good morning babe. Did you sleep well?"

"I slept okay."

"Are you hungry?"

"Yes, I am."

Martin fixed her a plate and placed it in front of her. He went back to the counter to grab his plate before taking a seat in front of Trina. He didn't want to think about the situation that happened yesterday before he met up with Tracy so he tried to direct the conversation in a more positive direction.

"Would you like to go see the new movie Straight Outta Compton? I heard it was awesome?"

"What time does it start?" Trina asked.

"I'm not sure, but after we finished breakfast, I'll check and let you know."

"I heard it took them almost five years to make this movie for one reason or another."

"Really, well no wonder it's getting great reviews."

"Out of curiosity, where did you go yesterday evening?"

"Damn, I knew this was coming," Martin thought to himself.

"I went to the Mall and then I went to have dinner with a friend. Why do you ask? Did something happen yesterday?" Trina looked at Martin, who had a smirk on his face.

"Oh no, nothing out of the ordinary happened yesterday, but I could have sworn I saw your car parked outside of Olive Garden."

Martin froze. What he couldn't understand was how she found his car.

"Cat got your tongue?" Trina asked jokingly.

"No, not at all. Kevin and I had dinner at Friday's in Castleton."

"Right."

After breakfast, Martin ran upstairs to check for movie times for Straight Outta Compton.

"Hey Trina, how does 2 sound?" Martin yelled.

"Two o'clock works for me."

Tracy moved her belongings downstairs to the guest room. She couldn't even stand the sight of Ron right now. She couldn't believe that Ron and Trina plan this entire thing just to get her pregnant and take her baby. Tracy now believes that Ron and Trina will try to make it look like she poisoned Ron and have her locked up and take her baby.

"Not in this lifetime, you motherfuckers," Tracy said as she looked down at her belly rubbing it.

Just then, Tracy heard a knock at her door. "Who is it?"

"It's Ron."

Tracy stood and walked over to open the door.

"What do you want Ron?"

"Hey, what's wrong?"

"Again, what do you want Ron?"

Ron moved his way inside the room. "We need to talk."

"Oh really and what about?"

"Us and the baby."

"Well the way I see it now there's no us, it's just the baby and me."

"Come on Tracy don't be like that I love you."

"No, you love Trina. I know what you two are up to and believe me it will not work."

"What the hell are you talking about?"

"Don't' play stupid with me Ron. I have already talked with detective Stevens and he said he talked with Trina and that her voice matched the voice on the recorder. So don't play any fucking games with me. You guys were going to try to frame me for poisoning you and take my baby away, bullshit, not today or any other day."

"Tracy I would never do that to you."

"I know this was Trina's plan and your stupid ass just went along with it, but there are people out there that know what you guys are trying to do and if anything happens to me, you guys are going down."

"Tracy baby you're not making any sense."

"Oh, I am making a lot of sense. You didn't think I would catch on to you guys, but I did and if you ever want to be in this child's life, you better stop whatever you and Trina are up to or I will make sure that you never see this child. Do I make myself clear? Oh, by the way, I need money to find a place to stay and get some things for the baby."

Ron stood there in disbelief. He was shocked that Tracy would think such things. He loved her dearly and no way was he in any scheme with Trina to take the baby away from her. Ron had to admit that he was a little curious to know if Tracy and Martin had been hooking up so whenever Tracy would leave, he would call Trina just to see if Martin was there with her.

"Tracy please have a seat there are some things I need to discuss with you, I want to come clean with you right now. I don't want you to leave this house. Believe me, I do love you and I would never do anything to harm you or the baby. If it will make you feel any safer, you can continue to stay here in the guest room, but if you're not in this house, I cannot protect you from anything that Trina might do to you. I know Trina believes you and Martin are seeing each other and she is very upset about it. I will be honest with you, when Trina found out that you were pregnant, she wanted to get back together with me and raised the baby together without you, but I wanted no parts of it. Trina wants a baby so bad, but she can never carry a baby full term. I do believe she set this all up leaving you and me alone together while she was with her girlfriends in LA. She hoped that we would get together and you would get pregnant, but once she was in LA, she had second thoughts about us being together and came home early, but by that time, it was too late, I had already fallen for you. I also believe she was trying to kill me and maybe you and I confronted her about it and she told me that if I went to the police with this that I would never see you are the baby so that's why I said it wasn't her voice on the tape recorder."

"Ron, why didn't you tell me this?" I was so hurt thinking that you two had planned to get rid of me."
Ron moved closer to Tracy, wrapped his arms around her, pulled her in closer to him and brushed his lips against hers.
"I love you, Tracy. Why would I ask you to marry me if I wanted you out of the way?"
Tracy leaned her head against Ron's chest and broke down uncontrollably.
With tears in her eyes, Tracy looked up at Ron. "When will your divorce be final?"

"I spoke with my attorney and he said it should be final within a few days."

"Great!"

After the movie, Trina and Martin went out for dinner. "How about I spend the night with you in the tent tonight?"

"Really?" Martin said suspiciously. He doesn't trust Trina anymore and wondered what she had up her sleeves.

"Yes, I think it will be fun just relaxing, all hugged up, listening to music and sipping on some wine."

"Um..." Martin said.

Later that night, Martin and Trina were lying on the blow-up mattress in the tent laughing and talking when Trina decided to undress him. Trina undressed Martin down to his socks. She opened her robe showing her assets causing Martin to rise up and flip her over on the mattress on her back.

"Damn, I thought I was a part of the WWA for a minute," Trina said.

Martin laughed. "Now open those legs for daddy," Martin said as he got down on his knees and buried his head between Trina's legs.

Martin slowly moved his tongue up and down her pussy applying pressure to each stroke. He then made his way down to her hole and with his tongue, he flicked it all around her and moved it in and out of her until she couldn't take it anymore.

"Oh, Martin baby please come inside of me."

Ten minutes later, Martin was fast asleep with Trina lying on his chest. Trina rose up and moved closer to Martin, just to make sure he was sleeping before heading inside the house. Trina eased off Martin, unzipped the tent and eased out, careful not to wake Martin. She slowly zipped it back up and made her way inside the house to her bedroom.

An hour later, Martin woke to a shadow standing over him with an object. He couldn't make out what the object was or if it was a female or a male standing over him, but when he tried to move, the stranger struck him in the head with the object that knocked him out. The next thing Martin's knew he was fighting to get out of the tent that was now on fire. He tried to unzip the tent, but was unable to, he cried out for Trina, but his cries went unheard. Martin frantically searched the tent for a sharp object when he saw through the smoke the corkscrew that he had used for the wine. He was able to slit the back of the tent and escape, but just as he made it to the side of the house, he collapsed.

The next-door neighbor saw the smoke coming from the backyard, called the fire department, and then ran over to make Trina aware of what was going on.

"Oh my God Trina said as she and the neighbor ran to the back. My boyfriend is in there." She cried out. "Let me go I have to get him out."

"No Trina you can't wait until the fire department gets here."

By the time the fire department arrived, the tent and all its belongings were burned. There was no sign of anything or anyone.

Trina was crying while her neighbor held her. The chief of police and the fire chief walked over to talk with Trina.

"Can we have a word with you inside?" The chief of police asked.

Inside Trina's home, the neighbor guided her to the loveseat and sat down beside her with his arm around her shoulder.

"I'm sorry for your loss Ms. Patterson."

"It's Mrs. Patterson. "

"I'm sorry. Our men will be working through the night collecting evidence. Your neighbor tells me that your boyfriend was inside the tent. Do you know what he was doing in the tent?"

"Yes, he was sleeping. I stayed out in the tent with him until he fell asleep and then I came inside and got in my bed. The next thing I remember is Marty knocking at my front door."

Do you have any idea how the fire would have started? Did your boyfriend smoke? Were there any objects in the tent that could have started the fire?"

"No. There was a blow- up mattress, a radio, an electrical cord and some lights, but it was turned off when I left."

"What was the young man's name that was in the tent?"

"His name was Martin Jackson," Trina said before bursting out in tears.

"Can you come down to the station tomorrow and give us a statement."

"Sure."

Just then, a young firefighter knocked on the front door. "Chief, can you come out back?" One of the firefighters asked.

The fire chief and police chief walked around the house to the backyard where some of his men met them.

"I didn't want to say anything in front of the lady, but we found her boyfriend's body on the side of the house. He was unconscious until we got him inside the ambulance and the paramedics had a chance to work on him when he told us that Trina Patterson tried to kill him. He also asked that we not let her know that he's alive."

"Are you sure that's what he said?"

"Yes, we're positive. They're taking him to Community North if you want to talk with him. Also, I found a club with blood on it and from the looks of the guy; it was used to knock him out."

"The guy's name is Martin Jackson and he is Mrs. Patterson's boyfriend. For his sake, let's keep this quiet until the morning. I have asked Mrs. Patterson to come down to the station tomorrow and give a statement so we will deal with it then, but first, I want to speak with Mr. Jackson." The chief of police said.

Hours later, and after everyone had left her backyard, Trina called Ron crying.

"Trina, what is going on?"

"Martin is dead. He died in a fire in a tent in my backyard."

"What! What was he doing in a tent?" Ron was so confused.

"What is it, honey?" Tracy asked.

"Trina said Martin is dead. She said something about him dying in a fire in a tent in her backyard. I think I need to head over there to see what she's talking about. Babe, you stay here and I will be right back."

"Trina I'm on my way over there."

"Why do you have to go?"

"Tracy I need to see what's going on. You said Martin was helping you get evidence on Trina, hell she could have killed him for all we know."

"Then you need to call the police and let them go over there. You need to stay out of it Ron."

Ron kissed Tracy on her forehead. "I'll be back shortly."

Hours went by and still no word from Ron. Tracy walked downstairs to the family room and peeked out the front window, hoping to see Ron's car pull up, but unfortunately, Ron hadn't shown up so Tracy marched upstairs, changed into her clothes and was out of the house in no time. She didn't know what was going on, but she was damn sure going to find out.

Tracy pulled into Trina's driveway. As she got out, she could smell the smoke from the fire. Her heart dropped to her stomach to think that Martin was dead.

Tracy knocked on the door several times before Ron and Trina opened the door. Trina was hanging onto Ron by the waist when he opened the door.

"Oh, I see it's like this now?" Tracy said sarcastically.

"It's not what you think Tracy," Ron said, moving Trina's arm from around him.

"No wonder you didn't want me to come over here with you. What the hell is going on Ron?"

"Baby look I came over here to see what was actually going and Trina said Martin burned in a fire tonight and since my name is on the deed to the house, I felt I needed to come over here to check things out. That is it, I promise."

"He's still my husband, I hope you know that and by the way Ron, did Tracy tell you that I caught her over here with Martin last month and from the smell of things I believe they were having sex. So now you worried about me and my husband. Yes, I fucked my husband. "

"Both of you can go straight to hell! What did you do to Martin, Trina? You knew he was on to your ass so you had to get rid of him. Well, just wait until I start talking."

"You better tell her Ron," Trina said.

"Tell me what? What are you going to do to me, set me on fire like you did Martin." Tracy said before heading back to her car. She was so pissed that she left before she slapped the shit out of Trina and Ron.

"I think I need to go home. I will check on you tomorrow Trina."

"Aw, so you just going to leave me here by myself?"

"I'm going home to my baby's mother."

On the ride home, Tracy cried like a baby, she was crying so hard that she never saw the car that ran the red light until it slammed into the driver's side of her car.

CHAPTER EIGHTEEN

Ron was on his way home when he approached a car accident. He slowly rode past the two-car collision thinking that the car looked just like Tracy's car and once he saw a woman that resembled Tracy, he felt as if he was going to pass out when the paramedics pulled the woman from the car.

Ron hoped out of the car and ran over to the body. "Oh my God Tracy, Oh baby please be okay!"

"Sir, I need for you to move so we can get her to the hospital."

"She's pregnant, she can't lose the baby."

"Come with me, sir." One of the paramedics asked Ron.

"So she's pregnant?"

"Yes."

"How far along is she?"

"I think about twenty weeks."

"And you are?"

"I'm her boyfriend."

"Can you follow us to the hospital?"

"I'll meet you there. Take her to Community North." Ron yelled out to the paramedic as he rushed to his car.

Ron pulled up the same time as the ambulance. He ran alongside the paramedics as they rushed Tracy inside.

"Sir this is as far as you can go. You can take a seat in the waiting area and we will have the doctor come out to speak with you." The nurse said to Ron.

Ron paced back and forth nervously when he overheard the nurse mention the name, Martin Jackson. The nurses were chatting about how handsome he was and how they admired his body.

"Martin Jackson," Ron said out loud. "But I thought he was dead."

By this time, Ron was so confused, but he couldn't focus on that right now, he wanted and needed to know that Tracy and the baby were going to be fine.

An hour later, the doctor greeted Ron. "I take it you're Mr. Patterson?"

"Yes, I am."

"I'm Doctor Reynolds. I must say Tracy and the baby are fine. You can thank God for that because there is no way Tracy or the baby should have come out of this accident unharmed. We would like to keep her overnight, but she should be free to go home in the morning."

"Are you serious? I saw the car and it's totaled."

"That's why I said you should thank God for protecting them."

"Can I go back and see her?"

"Sure the nurse just finished wiping the blood off of her face from her nose bleed."

Ron walked back to the room to find Tracy lying in bed with her eyes closed. He walked over to her and grabbed a hold of her hand.

"Hey Babe, how are you feeling?"

Tracy opened her eyes and looked at Ron. "I don't want you here."

"Tracy please don't be like that. I know now that I shouldn't have gone running over to Trina's to her rescue. I had a stupid moment what can I say and by the way, I never had sex with her."

Tracy turned over on her side facing the opposite side of Ron.

"You can be mad if you want, but I am not leaving here without you. I'm staying here until they release you."

"Suit yourself, but I don't want to talk to you right now."

"That's fine, you don't have to talk just as long as I know you and the baby are okay, that's good enough for me."

Ron pulled the covers back on the bed next to Tracy, got in and got under the covers, and relaxed his eyes.

A few minutes later, Tracy turned to see what Ron was doing since he was so quiet. When she turned, she found Ron asleep in bed with the covers pulled up to his neck. Tracy shook her head and turned back over with a smile on her face. "My baby's daddy," she said under her breath.

Martin asked one of the nurses that continued to come in his room for no apparent reason if he had heard right about them bringing in a Tracy Simmons and that she had been in a bad car accident.

"Yes, she was brought in late last night."

"Is she going to be okay?"

"God was watching over her. Her car was totaled and all she suffered was a bloody nose and her baby is okay as well. Oh, maybe I shouldn't have said anything."

"No, I won't say anything. Tracy is a dear friend of mine, but she can't know that I'm here."

"Your secret is safe with me. Is that the reason you have a couple of cops sitting outside your door?"

"Yes, but no one can know I'm here. That's all I can say."

Martin looked at the other nurse that was filling up his water picture and waited until she left before asking the other nurse to do him a favor.

"Hey, can you do me a favor?"

"Sure, what is it that you need?"

"I need to know what room number Tracy Simmons is in and her phone number."

"Let me find out for you and I will be right back."

Within minutes, the nurse was back with Tracy's room number and phone number.

"Whatever you do, do not tell anyone I gave this to you." The nurse said as she walked out of Martin's room.

The next morning Trina phoned Ron while he was at the hospital.

"Hello," Ron whispered.

"Why are you whispering?"

"I'm at the hospital?"

"Are you okay?"

"Yes, Tracy was in an accident last night after leaving your place."

"What do you want Trina?"

"You know what I want. I want you back and I want that baby."

"That's not happening and for your information, I told Tracy all about your little plan, so if anything happens to her, you will be the first person the police will come for," Ron said as he disconnected the call, got back under the covers, and dozed back off.

Tracy heard the ringing of Ron's phone and his conversation with Trina but pretended to be asleep. She couldn't believe Trina, she was such a lunatic. Tracy could not understand how Ron could have stayed married to someone like her. What type of hold did she have on him she wondered?

Tracy turned over to look at Ron. She smiled as she watched him all bundled up under the covers sleeping, hearing him snore lightly when the doctor walked in.

"Good morning, how are you feeling?"

"I'm so sore other than that, I feel fine."

"If that's all you feel after that type of car accident you were in, then I will say you are very blessed. Let's just say that the driver of the other car was not as blessed as you are. He died on the scene."

"Oh my God! Are you serious?"

"Very serious, his blood alcohol level was way above the limit."

"So when can I go home?"

"I'll have the nurse come in and do her rounds with you and if everything is good you will be free to go."

"Okay, thanks."

Two hours later, Tracy and Ron pulled into the driveway.

"You know what, with so much going on, I forgot to call Louise and let her know what had happened."

"Oh, she is going to be furious with you."

"I know."

Louise greeted the two at the door. "Where have you guys been?"

"Tracy was in a bad car accident last night and was rushed to the hospital."

"What and you didn't call to tell me."

"I'm so sorry with all that was going on, my mind was on Tracy and the baby."

Louise raised her hands to her mouth in disbelief. "Is the baby okay?"

"Yes, we're both fine," Tracy said.

"Oh, thank God," Louise said as she wrapped her arms around Tracy.

"You poor baby. Come on in here so I can fix you some breakfast."

"What about me?" Ron asked giving Louise his sad face.

"Aw come on you big baby."

Ron smiled as he helped Tracy inside the house and down the hall to the kitchen.

Louise prepared a huge breakfast for the three of them. They sat at the kitchen table for a couple of hours filling Louise in on everything about Trina and how Martin was killed in the fire.

"Oh, I almost forgot, I overheard some nurses talking about a Martin Jackson. They talked like he was still alive."

"Really, what did they say about him?"

"Just the usual like oh he is so fine and his body is tight." Tracy laughed.

"That's too funny."

"Oh, I heard about that this morning on the news, but they never said anything about a body. They just said there was a fire in the backyard."

Just then, the home phone rang.

"I'll get it," Louise said.

Louise answered on the third ring.

"Hello, hello, hello." Then the call was disconnected.

"Um… that was weird," Louise said as she made her way back to the table.

"What's wrong Louise?" Tracy asked.

"The call was from Community hospital, but no one said anything and then they just hung up."
Out of nowhere, something came flying through the patio window."

"Oh my God!" Tracy yelled as the sound of glass breaking and shattered on the kitchen floor, minutes later, they heard the sound of a car speeding off out front.
Tracy was so shocked and scared to death that she couldn't move. Ron and Louise rushed to the patio door to see what was going on when they noticed the brick.

"Ain't this a bitch! Someone just threw a brick through the patio window." Ron said in frustration.
Tracy was still sitting at the kitchen table. Ron walked over to her to see if she was okay because the look that she showed on her face was pure horror.

"Tracy, are you okay?" Ron asked. Then all of a sudden, Tracy starts crying.

"Why, why is this all happening? I am so scared Ron that something bad is going to happen. I don't feel safe anymore."

"Tracy honey, I will never let anyone hurt you if you don't believe anything, you can believe that."

"Ron just hold me please."

"Oh baby your shaking," Ron said as he wrapped his arms around her and kissed her on the forehead.

"I told you I am so scared."

"It's going to be all right. It will take more than someone throwing a brick through my window to scare me."
Ron had a feeling that the person behind this was no one other than his wife. She was mad because he told Tracy about her plan.

"Just wait until I get my hands on that bitch," Ron said under his breath.

"Ron I need to lay down."

"All right babe can you make it by yourself or do I need to carry you?"

"I think I can make it. I'm just so sore, but I'll take being sore over being dead any day."

"Well, I would hope so."

Ron and Tracy both burst out laughing.

Once Ron got Tracy settled in bed, he made his way back downstairs to the family room and called Trina.

"Hey Trina I know you're there and I know it was you who throw the brick through the patio window. Keep on fucking with me if want and you will be damn sorry." Ron told Trina and then disconnected the call.

Twenty minutes later, Ron gets a call from Martin.

"Hey, Ron this is Martin."

Ron hesitated to say anything. He was confused.

"I know everyone believes I'm dead, but I'm not. I'm only reaching out to you because I feel that you and Tracy are in danger. Trina will not stop until Tracy or you are dead if not the both of you. It's true, she tried to kill me and the police know all about it, but the one thing keeping them from arresting her is proof. I've been working with detective Stevens and they will be watching her so you cannot tell Trina anything."

"Man, I'm glad you're alive. I believe Trina came over here and threw a brick through the patio window this morning. I didn't see her, but something tells me it was her. A couple of months ago, she came to me after finding out Tracy was pregnant, she wanted to frame Tracy for trying to kill me and have her arrested so that Trina and I could raise the baby. I told Tracy all about it and this morning when Trina called me at the hospital, I told her I told Tracy and she was furious, so throwing a brick through my window was her payback."

"That sounds just like something Trina would do," Martin said.

After calling the police and calling someone out to replace the patio glass, Ron walked down the hall to find Louise. He wanted to let Louise in on what was going on and to tell her to be very careful and to watch her surroundings, and then he went upstairs with Tracy and lay down next to her, wrapped his arm around her and fell asleep.

CHAPTER NINETEEN

Trina's car was parked down the street from Ron's place after the brick was thrown through the patio window. She sat watching the house as detective Stevens and his partner watched her. He saw Trina running from the back of the house, jumping in her car and speed off, but he had no clue what she had just done, but what he couldn't understand was why she returned and why she parked down the street again.

"This lady is too fine to be so cruel. I cannot believe she tried to kill someone and set him on fire. Damn, all the fine ones are crazy as hell." He said to his partner.

Trina decided to head home, she had no idea that detective Stevens was watching her every move and had been doing so for a couple of days now, even before the fire.

Trina pulled into her driveway while detective Steven parked three houses down from her. He watched her as she walked inside the house. He wished he could hit that before he had to arrest her. She was fine as wine he thought. When he came over a few days ago and spoke with her, he was turned on just by the way she walked.

"Too bad that's all going to go to waste pretty soon. That's a damn shame." He said out loud.

"Let's just keep Charlie in your pants where he belongs and remember what our job is." His partner said.

"I know, but it's just a shame for someone so pretty to be this hateful. I wonder what triggered the hate in her."

"It's not our job to find that out, it's our job to prove that she is this crazy murderous person and if we can't do that, then who knows who will be her next victim and if you're not careful, you might be it."

"What are you talking about?"

"I know you hear what I'm saying, but somehow I don't believe you will take my advice and stay away from her. I see her as a challenge for you."

"Whatever I don't have time for challenges. I'm all about work right now." He said as he gave his partner a wink.

"You know you're making me think you're jealous. I know you secretly want to be with me. Go ahead and admit it."

"Jake Stevens you are crazy as hell. I just don't want my partner ending up in the morgue."

Ron was asleep lying next to Tracy when his cell phone rang. It rang three times before he knew it was his phone ringing. He rose up, reached over and grabbed his phone from the nightstand.

"Hello."

"Did you like your little present this morning?"

"Trina," Ron said as the caller disconnected the call. It didn't sound like Trina, but Ron couldn't be for sure. He went back and scrolled through his phone to see what the incoming number was coming from, but it wasn't Trina's number it was a number that he did not recognize. He dialed the number back, but he didn't get an answer. This puzzled Ron because he was so sure that this was Trina's' doing and if he was wrong, he owed her a big apology.

Ron sat in bed thinking when Tracy rose up. "What's wrong babe?"

"I just got a call on my cell phone. The caller asked me if I liked the present this morning. It didn't sound like Trina nor was it her number that the call came from."

"Are you serious? Who else could it be?"

"I don't know this is what puzzles me. This is so crazy, how did we get to this point where I'm being poisoned, someone throws a brick through my window, Trina threatened you and my baby to someone trying to murder Martin?"

Back at Trina's, she sat tied to a chair while someone disguised as she started walking back and forth, in front of her holding a gun.

"Just so you know your husband thinks it was you who throw the brick through his patio window this morning and the police believe it's you who killed Martin in the fire and it will be you who the police charge for the murder of Tracy, her unborn child, Ron, and Gloria. See Trina you had it all, but that was not good enough for you, you had to have Martin too. Martin and I were deeply in love, but you and all the others ruined that and when Tracy came along she took him further away from me, but both of you bitches will pay for what you did to me. I also know about your friend Gloria, but I put a stop to that ass from running behind Martin."

"What are you talking about? Martin is a no good for nothing fuck. He doesn't love anyone. Why would you waste the rest of your life over Martin he isn't worth it. He didn't love you or me for that matter."
Out of nowhere, she slapped Trina as hard as she could.

"How dare you say he didn't love me. He loved me until your nasty ass came into the picture and bought him all the things I couldn't. You think money can really buy you love, you dumb bitch?"

"Dumb, you're the dumb one. You're the one who will go to jail for murder for the rest of your life over a man who could care less about you. Oh, now I see you must be Cynthia. He told me all about you. He told me how you stalk him every day and night until he had to have a restraining order against you. Martin told me how awful you were in bed and how he felt sorry for you. Honey that was the only reason he hung around for as long as he did. You're pretty, but it takes more than a pretty face to keep a man like Martin. Face it, you didn't have what it took to keep him."

"You don't know what you're talking about. Take it back?" Cynthia yelled as she pointed the gun at Trina's head.

"Okay, okay I'm sorry. I just said that to make you mad."

"Bitch you don't know who you're fucking with. Why don't I fuck that husband of yours and see how that makes you feel? Oh, I forgot, he's not yours anymore and he likes young pretty women like Tracy and no old bitches like yourself.

"Fuck you, you stupid bitch," Trina yelled in anger. Cynthia laughed. "I see how to get you mad now. It's Ron you wanted not so much Martin, but what happened? Didn't you know how to keep your husband satisfied? I guess it took a younger person to satisfy him and carry his baby." That did it. Trina tried her best to get untied she wanted to slap that smirk off Cynthia's face.

"Temper, temper."

"Oh, by the way, did you ever think about who really tried to poison Ron? I know everyone believed you did, but guess who did it? I didn't do it on purpose I thought the water and coffee were for you. You know you should never leave your cart unattended at the grocery store. You gave me plenty of time to insert the poison into the bottles of vitamin water and into the coffee bag, but I had no idea that you were planning to do the same thing, but only you planned to make him sick and I planned to kill. It's a good thing Tracy got rid of the rest of the water and coffee before it was too late.

"What is it that you want from me?" Trina asked.

"Oh don't worry, I will get what I want from you, just like I got what I wanted from Gloria. Did you know that your friend was bisexual? Um… it makes me wonder if you are?"

"Hell naw I'm not bisexual I love men. Men like Martin Jackson."

"If I hear Martin's name come out your mouth one more time, I will kick the shit out of you."
Trina laughed. "Oh, I see how to get your nasty drawls in a knot."

"Whatever it is that you plan to do to me just do it and get it over with."
Just then, Cynthia pointed the gun to Trina's head and pulled the trigger."
Blood flew everywhere. "Bitch don't fuck with me," Cynthia said as she walked to the kitchen to rinse the blood off her face and hand.

"Three down, three to go," Cynthia said as she untied Trina and allowed her body to fall to the floor where she rolled her up in a black plastic bag.

Detective Stevens and his partner were sitting down the street when they thought they heard the sound of a gun go off.

"What was that?"

"It sounded like a gunshot to me. It had to come from one of these houses here."

"I know. I'll check this one and you check the other one. We can check Trina's house together."

Minutes later, after talking with both neighbors, they were certain that the gunshot had come from Trina's. Both detectives walked up the walkway with guns in hand.

"You check the back while I check the front." Detective Stevens told his partner.

Detective Stevens peered into the front window, he saw blood on the wall and at that point, he called for backup. Just then, his partner made her way around the front.

Cynthia noticed the two detectives so she eased her way out of the house through the backyard and ran to her car that was parked on the other street.

"Damn that was close," Cynthia said as she pulled off. She drove back to her place to plan her attack on Tracy, her unborn bastard, and Ron.

As backup arrived, detective Stevens and his partner approached the front door, gun in hand while the others ran around back. Detective Stevens knocked on the door several times calling out to Trina.

"Trina this is detective Stevens are you all right in there?" He called out again before turning the doorknob and to his surprise, the door was unlocked. As the two made their way inside the house, they moved further inside and to their right, they found something wrapped in a black plastic bag and saw blood splatter all over the wall.

Detective Stevens walked over, bent down, opened the bag and was heartbroken when he saw Trina.

"Oh my God! Not Trina. Damn who would do this to her?"

Trina still had a rope tied to one of her hands and to her ankles and a gunshot to her right side of her head.

Detective Stevens was so distraught that he had to walk outside. He walked over, stood by his car and turned to his partner.

"We need to go and talk with Ron and Tracy. This doesn't add up Trina did not kill herself so we have another suspect."

Fifteen minutes later, Detective Stevens and his partner pulled into Ron's driveway. They both hesitated getting out at first, but they had a job to do a job that was getting more complicated.

Louise answered the door and welcomed both detectives inside.

Ron, Tracy, and Louise sat in the family room with the detectives when they broke the news to them.

"Are you serious?" Ron said as he stood up.

"This is confusing because we saw Trina leave your home this morning and we watched her go inside her home. No one else entered, not through the front anyway."

"Are you sure it was Trina that you saw this morning? Because I got a phone call from someone who didn't sound like Trina and the call did not come from Trina's number asking me if I liked my present this morning."

"Well, we thought it was Trina. It was definitely her car, but we didn't actually see her face."

"So it could have been someone else driving her car?" Tracy asked.

"Yes."

"But who?" Ron asked.

"That's what we have to find out. I will assign a police car to sit outside your house. I have a feeling whoever it is, will try to do some harm to one of you or both."

Ron paced back and forth. He could not believe someone had murdered Trina and tried to kill Martin.

"So you think whoever has done this will come for us?"

"I don't know, but I would rather be safe than sorry." Just then, the doorbell rang.

"Let me get that." Detective Stevens said.

"Who are you and where's Ron?" Rene asked as she pushed her way into the house. "Get out of my fucking way, Ron," Renee yelled.

"It's okay, she's a friend of the family."

"Ron, what's going on? I heard on the news that there was a murder at Trina's and when I went over there they wouldn't tell me anything."

Renee sits down. "Trina was murdered sometime today."

"No Ron don't say that," Renee said as she stood. "Trina is not dead." She said as the tears began to fall. Ron hugged Renee and tried to comfort her.

"It's true Renee," Louise said as she moved closer to Renee. Someone tried to murder Martin as well."

"What! What is going on here?" Should I be worried?" Renee asked.

"I don't believe so." Detective Stevens said.

Renee grabbed her phone and dialed Gloria's number, but she got no answer.

"I need to go and tell Gloria. I will be right back." Renee headed over to Gloria. As she turned the corner, she spots her car in the driveway. "I guess she's still mad at me." Renee thought this was the reason Gloria didn't answer her call.

Renee knocked at the door and the door opened slightly. She moved further into the house, but the odor almost knocked her down.

"Gloria, what the hell is going on with this smell?" Renee said as she walked down the hall to Gloria's bedroom where she saw Gloria tied to the bed butt naked.

"What the fuck!" Renee moved closer and almost gagged from the smell and the sight of Gloria with a bullet to her head.

Renee screamed repeatedly, "No, not you too. Help me, somebody help me." Renee screamed, running out of the house over to the next-door neighbor's house where she collapsed right before telling them that Gloria was dead. When Renee came to, the entire block was crawling with police cars, the paramedics, and several news reporters. Renee looked through the crowd and saw detective Stevens, Ron, and Tracy. She turned to her left and saw Gloria being carried out in a body bag. She couldn't get the sight of Gloria's dead body out of her head.

Renee sat in the ambulance in a daze as detective Stevens approached her.

"How you're holding up?"

"Am I next? Renee asked.

"Let's hope not."

"Do I need to leave town or something?"

"No, if you leave town, we can't protect you. We will assign a couple of officers to you. They will sit out front of your home or in your driveway whichever you prefer."

"Great."

Tracy walked over to Renee. "This is so crazy. I feel like I'm in a movie or something. Renee whatever you do, please be careful."

"We all need to be careful, especially you since you're pregnant."

"Yeah, that's what worries me the most because I want so bad to be a mom and a good one at that. What happens if I die before I can give birth? Then my life would have been nothing but a waste."

"Don't say that Tracy. I'm sure the last couple of months was wonderful for you."

Tracy looked over at Ron. "You're right, it has. I have Ron to thank for that. We're getting ready to head home, if you need anything please let us know or if you want to stay with us until this person is caught you can."

"Thank you, Tracy."

"Take Care." Tracy said as she walked over to Ron's car."

Ron and Tracy headed back home to be with Louise and to go over plans for Trina's funeral. Louise had taken Trina's death hard. She and Trina have known each other for over 20 years and now to learn that Gloria was dead, it was just too much for her.

"Ron I have a feeling that bad things are just starting and that there will be more to come and I am scared to death. I have never been so happy in all my life here on earth and to feel that it's coming to an end is so heartbreaking. I love you Ron and I don't want to lose you or be taken away from you."

Ron patted Tracy's knee. "Babe everything is going to be fine. Stop thinking negative and think positive."

"Hell thinking positive won't stop a fool from trying to kill you if they want you dead. Someone tried to kill Martin. They killed Trina and Gloria now Renee, you, Louise and I could be next. Who from their past would want them dead? What we need to do is find out is who is the common denominator between us all. I would say Martin is the common denominator and the way he changes women it could easily be one of his crazy women that he has done wrong."

CHAPTER TWENTY

When Ron and Tracy made it home and was inside the house, Ron called detective Stevens to tell him what Tracy thought about the killings and asked him to come over so they could sit down and talk.

When detective Stevens and his partner Celeste arrived, they noticed a black tinted car parked across the street from Ron's.

The detectives got out and walked over to the unmarked car and had a conversation with the cops assigned to watch Ron's home about the car, but just as they finished their conversation and looked over at the car, the person driving the car pulled off.

"If that car is seen again, find out who the driver is," Ron told the two cops assigned to Ron's house.

Detective Stevens and Celeste walked inside Ron's home. They found all parties sitting in the family room waiting for them. They took a seat on the loveseat and Tracy began to tell them what she thought about the situation.

"You know this could be true. It all started with Martin and all of you have had some kind of relationship with him except for Renee, Louise, and Ron."

"All shit don't say that. That means I'm next."

"Well, we are going to make sure that doesn't happen. I need to speak with Martin about his past relationships and asks if he thinks this could be possible."

"Here you can call him from here?" Ron said as he dialed Martin's number and handed the phone to the detective.

Detective Stevens spoke with Martin, but Martin couldn't think of anyone right off the back that would be this damn crazy.

"All I ask of you three is to be very careful when you go somewhere don't go by yourself. Stick together, you will be safer in a group of three or two than to be alone. Ms. Louise, I really don't think you have anything to worry about, but just in case, be careful until we catch this person."

Later that evening, Renee showed up. She didn't want to be alone now that her best friends were dead.
Ron saw Renee walking up and walked to the door to let her in.

"Can I come and join you guys?"

"Sure, come on in. We're sitting out back on the deck. Have you had dinner?"

"No, I haven't even thought about it."

"Go in the kitchen and fix yourself a plate and join us on the deck."

"Thanks, Ron."

"No problem."

Renee walked into the kitchen, grabbed a plate and started piling shit on her plate. She was starving since she hadn't had food all day. She was just getting ready to fix breakfast when she found out about Trina.

"You know being here around you guys make me feel so much better. I feel Trina's presences all around here."
Tracy looked over at Renee.

"Thanks, Renee, that's just what I wanted to hear."

"I'm sorry Tracy."

"Just so you know Renee. I will be going to the funeral home tomorrow to make funeral arrangements for Trina. And by you being one of her best friends, you are welcome to come with us."

"Thanks Ron for letting me be a part of this. I know Trina would want her friends to help out." Renee said right before crying. "I'm sorry guys, but this is so hard. I have lost two of my best friends today. I feel so alone."
Tracy got up, walked over to Renee and hugged her.

"We understand, but don't feel alone we are here for you. Whatever you need, you just let us know and the offer still stands if you want to stay with us for a while."

"Thank you so much, Tracy."

After Martin's release from the hospital, he was so hurt when he found out that Trina and Gloria were murdered. After talking with the detective, he had wrecked his brain trying to think of anyone from his past that would do something like this. He had a feeling that these murders did have something to do with his past, but he couldn't put his finger on the one person that could be responsible.

Martin drove over to Ron's, he wanted to let him know how sorry he was for the loss of his wife. As Martin walked up the walkway to Ron's front door, he felt funny being there. He had spent so many good times here with Trina, Tracy, and Ron. He wished he could go back and do things differently and just maybe Trina and Gloria would be alive today.

Martin knocked twice before Louise answered the door.

"Hello, Martin what are you doing here?"

"I came to speak with Ron."

"Okay, come on in. We are all in the back on the deck."
Martin followed Louise to the back.

"Hello," Martin said as he made is way out on the deck.

"Ron can I speak with you in private"

Ron stood up and walked toward Martin, "we can talk in my study."

Ron and Martin walked to the study when they heard a knock at the door. When Ron opened the door he almost fainted, there stood a woman on his front porch who resembled Trina. This woman could have been her twin.

"Hello, Ron I just wanted to drop off this flower arrangement. I am so sorry for your loss."

"Why thank you. And who might you be?"

"I'm a longtime friend of Trina's and Gloria's."

"Okay, would you like to come in?"

"No, I just wanted to drop these off, but thanks anyway."
Martin heard the woman and recognized the voice, but he couldn't put a face to the name. He stepped out into the hall to try to get a glimpse of this woman, but Ron blocked his view.

As Martin moved closer, Ron closed the door and turned to see Martin standing there. He felt a certain way having Martin stand so close to him. He was so close he could smell the hospital scent on him still. Ron could feel the heat from Martin's body.

"Is something wrong?" Ron asked Martin as Ron touched Martin's hand.

"Yes, I recognized that voice. Who was that?" Martin asked as he backed away from Ron.

"I don't know. She said she was a longtime friend of Trina's and Gloria's."
This was unsettling to Martin. "I don't feel right about that lady. There's something about her voice that makes me believe she's someone from my past, but I don't know who. I wish I could have seen her."

"Well, she looked so much like Trina," Ron said.

"Really, what did she want?"

"She came to give her condolences and to drop off these flowers."

"Man you guys should be more careful when you open the door. This is probably how Trina and Gloria were murdered in their own home opening the door to strangers."

"Yeah, you're right. So what did you want to talk with me about?"
Martin licked his lips, trying to block out the feelings that were running through his body as he stood there looking at Ron.

"I just want to tell you how sorry I am about Trina and about everything. I know we had a good relationship while I worked here and it was foul of me to have an affair with your wife."

"Yeah, you were pretty foul, but if it wasn't you, it would have been someone else, but I all I have to say, is that you better stay the fuck away from Tracy or I will kill you for messing with her."
Martin threw up his hands. "I know Tracy is off limits but is she the only person who is off limits? Martin gave Ron a little wink.

Ron looked at Martin, as he thought back to their little escapade a year ago, and smiled. "You haven't changed a bit I see."

"Oh, I 'we changed all right, I've gotten better."

"Really?"

"Would you like to find out?"

Ron walked over to the entryway of his study and stuck his head out.

"Martin I don't want Tracy finding out about our little fling. Do I make myself clear?"

"Clear as water, but you didn't answer my question?"

"Martin don't, I can't do that to Tracy and as much as I would love to have sex with you, it can't happen again."

"Okay, but if you change your mind, let me know. By the way, I wanted to let you know that I do believe the murders are related to someone from my past. I can't put my finger on the person just yet, but when I heard the woman's voice at the door, the hairs on the back of my neck stood straight up. I wish I could have gotten a view of her."

"Like I said, she looked like Trina's twin."

"Um…" Martin began to think of all the women he had been involved with and who he hurt the most when he broke it off."

Then out of nowhere, the name Cynthia came to his mind. "Oh shit, I know who it could be. I dated here a couple of years ago and she told me that whomever I dated after her she would kill. She told me if she couldn't have me, no one would."

"Let me get the detective on the phone," Ron said.

The detective came back over to Ron's, he was determined to catch this person at any cost, but when he pulled into the driveway, he noticed the unmarked car was nowhere in sight. He got on his phone immediately and called his boss. He was told that the department could not afford to have the two detectives protect the house anymore.

"Damn, that's too bad because they believe the person behind this just showed up and delivered some flower arrangements."

"Why don't I have you assigned to the house?"

"You know I can't do that boss. As much as I would like to, I can't."

The detective walked up and knocked on the door. This time Ron didn't just open the door as he had been doing in the past.

"Who is it?" Ron asked.

"It's detective Stevens."

Ron peered out the family room window to verify who was at the door.

Ron walked over and opened the door.

"I see you're talking a precaution which is smart."

"Yeah, especially since the woman appeared at my door."

Ron, Martin, and detective Stevens sat in his study talking. Ron gave him the description of the woman and Martin supplied the name and possibly the reason behind her motives.

"Do you know where she lives?"

"No, I thought she left town, but who knows."

"I did see a black car parked across from here earlier today. The windows were tinted so I couldn't see who was driving."

"Hey, wait a minute, the lady that dropped off the flowers was in a black car with tinted windows."

"Come to think of it, Cynthia does resemble Trina. I bet that's reason I thought it was Trina that tried to kill me."

"I need to talk to everyone here. There's something I need to ask you guys." The detective said.

Ron, Martin, and the detective head out onto the deck.

"Hey, can I get your attention for a minute. I believe the person who committed these murders was the same person responsible for throwing the brick through the window and the same person who not too long ago dropped off the flower arrangements. So I need you to make sure you guys keep your eyes and ears open and if anything seems strange, do not hesitate to contact me or the police department. I would also like to see if it's possible to have all of you guys under one roof for a while?

"There's plenty of room here for everyone," Ron said.

"Detective Stevens, can you stay with us?" Tracy asked. They all laughed, but Tracy was serious.

"Are you serious Tracy?"

"I'm dead serious. You can laugh if you want, but I will not sleep knowing that there's someone out there that want to harm one of us."

"Aren't Ron and I enough protection?"

"You're not the part of the police department. As long as this person knows the detective is here, they won't dare try to come inside and harm one of us."

"Hell, if she's crazy, she won't care," Louise said as she got up, gathered the plates and made her way inside. While inside the kitchen, Louise kept hearing a crackling sound. "What is that?" She said out loud. Louise followed the sound that led her down the hall to the front door. She was a little hesitant to open, but decided she needed to know where the sound was coming from. When she opened the door, she was not prepared for what she saw. In the driveway was the detective's car burning.

"Oh my God!" Louise yelled.

Louise ran back to the others to let them know what was going on.

Detective Stevens was pissed. He got on the phone and called it in.

"This bitch is messing with the wrong person." He shouted! He then turned back around and out of the corner of his eye, he saw the black car slowly pull out of the driveway across the street and make its way down the street. Detective Stevens ran after the car to get the license number. Minutes later, detective Stevens called the dispatcher and asked if she could run the license plate numbers through the system, but unfortunately, nothing came back.

"Shit! I am so fucking mad right now. I'm glad this is the company car and not my own."

In no time, the street was flooded with cop cars, fire trucks, and the new stations.

Detective Stevens was standing there in shock as his boss walked up to him.

The lieutenant walked over and patted detective Stevens on the shoulder.

"Sir, we have got to give this family some protection. Hell, when they start setting police cars on fire, this lets you know that you're dealing with a psychopath. I will not sleep at night knowing this family is not protected."

"You're right, I will assign at least three officers to the house."

"I'm pretty sure the owner will make room for the officers in his home."

"Great, I will send them right over."

"Thanks, Lieutenant. I'll let the family know."

CHAPTER TWENTY-ONE

Later that night, Renee and Martin agreed it was for the best to be under one roof than to take any chances being alone making it easier for the killer to attack. Minutes later, three plain-clothes officers arrived and Ron showed them to their rooms. The house was full, but Tracy was still not satisfied. She wanted this person caught.

By ten o'clock, everyone had retired to their room. Ron, of course, was knocked out, but Tracy was too paranoid to sleep. Every little sound she heard had her up looking out of the window. It didn't matter that there were five male figures in the house. Tracy walked to the door, open it and stuck her head out just to see if she heard any noise when she thought she heard something downstairs coming from the kitchen. Tracy grabbed one of Ron's baseball bats and made her way out into the hall. She moved slowly down the hall to the stairs, creped down each stair and ran right into Martin who was coming out of one of the guest bedrooms that was at the end of the stairs. Tracy ran right into his hard shirtless body.

"Oh shit!" Tracy said before Martin caught her before she fell to the ground from the impact of running into his chest.

"And where are you off to with your bat?" Martin asked as he laughed while still holding her close to his body. Tracy broke away from Martin. Being that close to him did things to her. "I thought I heard some noise coming from the kitchen.

"Oh, that was me. I was reheating some food in the microwave. Would you care to join me?"

"Well, I am kind of hungry."

"Come on, let's go eat."

Martin watched as Tracy walked to the kitchen. Being pregnant was good for her. Her ass was bigger and her breast Oh my God he thought. Martin grabbed her ass cheek just to see how she would react.

"Now why did you do that?"

"Because I want to feel that phat ass."

"How would you feel if I just walked up and grabbed your dick?"

"Oh baby don't talk to me like that, but you do know that you can grab anything on my body anytime you want." Martin looked down at her breast as he did, he saw that her nipples were hard. He slowly ran his finger across one of her nipples and when she didn't say anything, he pulled her closer to him and kissed her on the lips.

"Oh Tracy baby, I have missed you so much. I missed licking your pussy." He said as he ran his hand between her legs.

"Martin please don't do this."

"Walk away then." He said as he waited for her to move away and when she didn't, he kissed her again. This time he deepened the kiss as he rubbed her breast.

Unable to resist his touch, Tracy ran her hand down the front of Martins pajamas.

"Oh, I see someone's excited," Tracy said, looking up at him.

"I want a little of that pregnant pussy," Martin said as he backed Tracy into the storage room on the side of the kitchen.

"Martin we can't. Martin please."

"Oh, I'm going to please you all right."

"Martin no!"

"Just let me stick the head in and then I will pull out just like that."

Martin parted Tracy's legs with his leg, pulled her panties to the side and slowly inserted the head in. The feel of her tight pussy made it difficult for him to pull out so he inched his way deeper inside of her and moved slowly in and out. He grabbed her bottom lip with his mouth and began to suck on it as the feeling of her wet pussy took control of him.

"Damn baby your pussy feels so damn good. Aw shit, Tracy slow it down baby, I don't want to come this quickly."

"Let me lay down on the floor it will make it easier," Tracy said.

Tracy lay down on the floor and Martin inserted himself inside of her. She felt warm, wet and tight. Martin was losing control of himself so he removed his dick and buried his head between her legs.

"Oh, Martin baby that shit feels so damn good."

"You better be quiet before someone hears us."

"Martin baby, I want to feel that big thick dick inside me now!"

"All right baby you want big Sal you got it."

Martin eased inside of her slowly. He was a little afraid that he somehow might hurt the baby.

"Now is that what you wanted?"

"Yes, baby yes," Tracy said right before Renee walked in the kitchen.

"Martin where are you? I thought you were getting some food for us?"

"What the fuck," Tracy whispered as she slapped Martin's face.

"Get off of me and get out of here."

Martin and Tracy stood and waited for Renee to leave the kitchen before exiting the storage room.

"I can't believe you," Tracy said as she exited the kitchen and headed back upstairs.

The next morning Ron and Tracy were sitting at the kitchen table eating breakfast when Martin and Renee walked in. Ron looked up and glared at Martin and Martin smiled.

"Good morning all," Martin said as he took a seat across from Tracy.

Ron said good morning to the two while Tracy continued to eat not even looking up at them.

"How would you guys feel if I grilled some steaks and burgers for dinner tonight?"

"That sounds good to me." Ron and Louise said.

"So Renee did you sleep alone last night?" Tracy asked.

Ron almost choked on his juice. "Was that necessary?"

"Oh, I'm sorry I was just thinking out loud."

Martin chuckled to himself. It made his morning to know that Tracy was jealous because she thought he and Renee slept together. Ron pretended not to notice how Martin was looking at Tracy and how uncomfortable she was at this very minute.

"Did something happen that I should know about?"

"No, not really. Martin and I kept each other company last night, that's all." Renee said.

Tracy rolled her eyes as she looked up at the ceiling.

"Ron, what time are we going to the funeral home?" Louise asked.

"I made an appointment for 11. Tracy, are you and Renee coming with me and Louise?" Ron asked.

"I'm coming because I am not staying here without you," Tracy said.

"I want to come," Renee said.

"Can I come?" Martin asked.

"Sure, but I would like for you to disguise yourself just in case that crazy lady is watching the house."

"We agree. We will follow behind you guys." The three officers said as they walked in the kitchen.

"Great you guys are just in time for breakfast," Louise said as she handed them their plates.

"Um, everything smells good." One of the officers said.

"Has anyone been outside this morning?" The second police officer asked.

"No, we haven't. Tracy replied.

"We will do a walk around right after breakfast just to make sure nothing has been vandalized."

At Ten thirty, everyone gathered in Ron's car as the officers got in their car and headed in the direction of the funeral home.

"This is something that I didn't think I would ever have to do," Ron said.

"I know. I still can't believe it." Louise said.

"Did you call your brother and his wife to let them know?" Tracy asked Ron.

"I forgot all about it. Baby, can you remind me when we get back to the house to call Kurt and Stephanie?"

Inside the funeral home, the three officers stood by the entrance while the others headed down the hall.

"Ron you guys can go in I'll wait out here," Tracy said.

"Are you sure?"

"Yes."

Ron and the others gathered in the room and discussed the funeral arrangements before picking out the casket. Tracy really didn't want to be a part of this because she just didn't feel right since Trina and Ron were still married and she's having his baby and living in Trina's and Ron's home. So she decided to stay behind the scene.

Forty-five minutes later, the funeral arrangements had been made and the casket had been chosen. The gang was ready to head out when the officers told them to wait. "We need to make sure the coast is clear."

"Is this necessary?" Renee asked.

"Yes, it is. What if you walk out there and someone walks up and shoots one of us?" Tracy said.

"All right, it's okay for you guys to leave.

Cynthia watched as the group was escorted to their car. She was parked across the street in an empty parking lot watching their every move. When they pulled off, so did she. She stayed three cars behind them so she wouldn't be noticed, but at this point, she didn't care who saw here she wanted Ron and Tracy's ass dead. She knew all about Ron and Martin's fling. Cynthia was determined to murder everyone that had been in contact with Martin. Cynthia felt she was doing society a favor by destroying the HIV spreaders.

She had contracted HIV from Martin about three years ago, and to this day, he is still running up in women and not telling them that he has the virus. She felt as though her life had been ruined. Cynthia believed that since she had the virus, no man would come near her and that was the one thing that she wanted in life was to be married and have kids, but Martin took all that away from her when he did not tell her about him being HIV positive.

That evening Ron decided to go into the office to get some files so he could work from home.

"Ron honey, I don't think it's a good idea for you to leave by yourself."

"Sweetheart, I will be fine."

Tracy tried talking to the officers in hopes of them talking some sense into him.

"I will follow Ron while the others stay here." The one officer said.

"Thanks that will make me feel much better. Ron make sure you come right back, okay babe."

"Yes, mother I will come right back." He said jokingly as he kissed her on the lips.

"Oh, before you leave, did you call your brother?"

"Yes, he's on his way back. He should be here sometime tomorrow."

When Ron walked out, the first thing he noticed was his car. The car tires were all flat.

"Ain't this a bitch," Ron said in frustration as he walked back into the house.

"That stupid witch has flattened all my tires."

"See I told you, you didn't need to go," Tracy said.

"You guys stay put." The officers walked outside and looked around for any signs of the black car. They walked around the house to see if there was any damage to the house.

"It looked like they just targeted the car. I'm going to call this in."

After he got off the phone with the dispatcher he was told that detective Stevens had just put out an ABP on a black town car with tinted windows and license plate number 3875psk."

"Why don't we leave and go to the beach house after the funeral. I would feel much better if we did." Tracy suggested.

Martin giggled as he looked at Tracy and licked his lips. Renee nudged Martin right after he did that. "What was that for?" She asked.

"What are you talking about? Just because I gave you a piece of this last night doesn't mean you're my lady so don't start acting like it." Martin whispered into her ears as he rolled his eyes.

Renee looked over at Tracy and rolled her eyes at her. Tracy shook her head but smiled on the inside.

"That would be too expensive." One of the officers said.

"Not really. We could use the companies Jet if we needed." Ron said.

"Not sure if the boss will approve that, but I can check to see what he has to say."

"Okay, so we can all plan to leave right after the funeral," Tracy said.

The next day, Ron's brother and sister -in- law arrived at the airport around 6 pm. One of the police officers was there to take them to the house. Ron had sneaked out of the house and used Martin's car to go into the office. He made sure the office was clear before he entered. The last thing he wanted to do was to endanger anyone in his company.

Ron took the elevator to the 12th floor. As the doors opened, he got a weird feeling that he was not alone. Ron looked at his surroundings before heading down the hall to his office. Once he opened the office door, he got the surprise of his life, he stood face to face with the woman who had delivered the flower arrangements.

"What the fuck are you doing in my office?" Ron yelled.

"Calm the fuck down," Cynthia said as she pulled out her gun.

"You and I both know why I'm here. You see, you fuck Martin many of nights while he worked as your Gardner. Martin was the man that I fell in love with. Martin was the man that destroyed my life so I'm eliminating every person that has been exposed to Martin. I want to stop you guys from spreading that nasty ass virus."

"What are you talking about?"

"I guess you don't know. Martin is HIV positive and is spreading that disease to people without their knowledge and in return, they are spreading it to people they come in contact with because they don't know, but I'm putting a stop to this right now. Trina, Gloria, Tracy, You and I will make sure I kill Martin's ass this time."

"Cynthia it doesn't have to be like this. You can expose Martin to the authorities."

"It's too late for me, I have already committed two murders."

Ron walked slowly toward Cynthia as he spoke with her. "Please don't do this Cynthia I have a baby on the way. Something I have wanted my entire life."

As Ron took his last step, Cynthia pulled the trigger striking Ron right dead in his forehead. She knew if she continued to listen to Ron, she would have had a change of heart. Cynthia stumbled back against the table. She was weak from the virus. The doctors had given her only six weeks to live. She was on her fourth week, too much work to do in such little time she thought.

Cynthia sat down for a minute to rest before heading to the ladies room to wash the blood from her face and hands. The virus was really starting to take a toll on her body. Her breathing was not good and she couldn't get rid of this cold she had. She began to sweat tremendously.

CHAPTER TWENTY-TWO

Several hours later, Tracy was frantic when she could not find Ron. His brother and sister-in-law had been there for at least an hour, but they were unable to locate him. Tracy called his cell phone several times but got no answer.

"Where could he be?" Tracy asked as she began to pace back forth in the kitchen when Martin pulled her aside.

"I let Ron use my car to go to his office."

"Why would you do that Martin?"

Tracy walked out of the kitchen and down the hall to the family room.

"Martin let Ron use his car so he could go into the office. I'm worried about him since he's not answering his phone. I need to use someone's car so I can go check on him."

"I'll take you," Kurt said.

"No, we will go and check on Ron." The officer said. "Just give us the address."

Twenty minutes later, the officers arrived at the location. They spotted Martins car along with several other cars parked in the parking lot. As they exited the car, they looked around the parking lot, but nothing seemed out of the ordinary. They made their way inside the building to the 12th floor and began to search the offices for Ron.

"Hey, Tom why don't you check the offices on the left and Larry you check the offices on the right while I check these rooms upfront." Joe the older officer said.

Joe checked the first office and as he opened the second door, he stood there for a second or two before saying anything. "He's over here, but it's not good."

Back at the house, Tracy was frantic, she could feel that something was not right. "Why haven't they called us yet?"

"Calm down Tracy. Why don't you take a seat." Kurt said.

"I can't sit until I know Ron is okay."

Then the phone rings, Tracy looks at the phone afraid to answer for fear of hearing the unbearable news.

Kurt gets up off the couch, walked over to the phone, and picked it up on the sixth ring.

"Hello, the Patterson's residence."

Is this Mr. Patterson?" The officer asked.

"Yes, it is."

"Well, I have some bad news. We just found Ron and he has been shot… in the forehead. He died on the scene."

When Kurt hung up the phone and turned to face Tracy, she could tell it was bad because Kurt's face was as white as an egg.

"Ron's dead."

"No, no, no don't you say that!" Tracy screamed before passing out.

Later, when she came to, Tracy looked around the room at everyone and hoped what she thought she heard Kurt say was just a dream.

"Kurt where's Ron?" Tracy asked.

"Baby Ron's gone."

Tracy cried in Kurt's arm, "Why, God, why would you take him from me. He was the only person who cared and loved me for me. Why God, why?"

Louise sat on the couch like a zombie. She couldn't believe this was happening. Things like this only happened in the movies, she thought.

Hours later when the officers arrived at the house, they were hesitant to tell Tracy what they found out, but being as serious as it was, they felt they had to. Joe sat down with everyone and read the note that was left behind on Ron's desk.

To all the HIV positive carriers:

Martin, Ron, Trina, Gloria, Tracy and Renee: Martin has infected all of you through sexual contact. He continues to infect people so I am eliminating those people so no one else has to go through what I am going through. Martin has ruined my life so that no other man will ever want me. I wanted the husband, the family, and the white picket fence, but because of Martin and his virus, I will never have that. Tracy out of all people, I feel for you the most because of the child that you carry that may be infected as well. It will hurt me the most when I kill the both of you. Martin, you have escaped death once, but not twice baby boy I'm coming for you. Ron and Martin had a sexual contact about a year ago and Trina, Gloria, and Renee all had sex with the Martin so you must all die and then I will join you all in hell!

The room was so quiet you could hear a pin drop. Louise sat with her mouth wide open as Kurt and his wife sat in disbelief.

"Is it true Martin? Are you fucking everyone passing on the virus?" Tracy asked in a calm matter.

"No, that's not true. She continues to tell people that I infected her, but I've been tested and I am HIV negative. So she has the wrong person. We need to stop her before she kills any more people."

"Martin you are the only person that knows her. Tell us more about her like where does she live and does she have any family, where does she work and where she could be hiding out at." Larry asked.

"I can't answer those questions. I have never met any of her family, we just had a sexual relationship we only got together to have sex and that was it. There was not a lot of talking, nor did we ever spend the night together. We did not date, we had no dinners, movies or anything like that. I hate to say this, but she basically paid me for sex."

"So this woman is killing everyone because she thinks you gave her HIV?" Kurt asked. Tears began to roll down Kurt's face. He came to help bury his sister- in- law, now he has to bury his brother. His heart ached because Ron was his only sibling.

"Did you sleep with my brother?" Kurt asked.

Martin looked over at Tracy. He hated to have her hear what he had to say about him and Martin, but it was out now so he had to come clean with everything.

"Martin and I had a sexual encounter one time about a year ago."

"So my brother was bi-sexual."

"You stop it right now! Don't you dare say that about Ron! Ron was not gay and you know that Martin." Tracy said before she got up. "I will not continue to sit here and listen to this bullshit."

Tracy walked out of the family and headed upstairs to her room. Once inside her bedroom, Tracy sat in the rocker for a couple of minutes. She got up and walked over to the dresser. She pulled open the dresser, dug underneath the clothes and pulled out a revolver. Tracy walked back over to the chair and sat thinking about everything that had happened. There was no way she wanted to live without Ron. She slowly put the gun up to the side of her head and pulled the trigger back, but right before she let go of the trigger something cause her arm to move a little.

The family room went quiet as the sound of a gunshot went off. Martin was the first person to run upstairs to the bedroom and then Kurt. Louise could not move she was still in shock after learning about Ron. The detectives followed.

"Call 911," Martin yelled.

Tracy had missed the side of her head by an inch, but it glazed the front of her forehead and knocked her out.

That night Tracy lay in the hospital bed crying her heart out. She cried for Ron and her unborn child because she will never get the opportunity to meet her wonderful father. While she was in the hospital, she asked to be tested for HIV. Her doctor decided to keep Tracy overnight to keep an eye on her mental health. They knew she was going through a rough time right now, and they didn't want her to try to harm herself again. God was with her tonight because this could have turned out much different.

The next morning, Tracy opened her eyes and tried to figure out where she was until the pain from her forehead caused her to remember. The pain was much worse than it was last night. Tracy rose up and noticed Martin asleep in the chair. She wondered to herself if he had been there the entire time.

"Martin, Martin," Tracy called out to him.

Martin opened his eyes to see Tracy staring at him. "Is everything okay?" he asked as he got up from the chair and rushed to her side.

"My head aches so bad."

"Call the nurse to see if she can give you something to ease the pain."

"I just rang her. Were you here all night?"

"Yes, I was. You didn't think I was going to let you stay here by yourself, did you?"

All at once, she remembered Ron and burst out crying.

"Tracy I know losing Ron is hard. You can cry as much as you want, but just know that I will always be here for you and that little girl of yours. Kurt and Stephanie will go and make funeral arrangement for Ron today. He felt it would be best to have Trina's and Ron's funeral together. I hope that doesn't offend you."

"No, that's fine."

Just then, the nurse came in with medication for her and the doctor was with her.

"Ms. Simmons I have some great news for you."

Then he noticed Martin.

"Tracy can I have a word with you in private." The doctor looked at Martin as he spoke.

"Whatever you have to say you can say it in front of him."

"Your HIV test results came back negative. You are not infected with the virus. If you don't mind me asking, why did you think you were carrying the virus?"

"Oh, it's a long story doc. I'm just glad that I don't have it."

"That makes two of us," Martin said as he grabbed hold of her hand.

The doctor left the room and Martin moved closer to Tracy.

"I need to tell you more about Ron and me, it's not what you think. It was a dare, he lost and we had to have sex. It only happened once and neither one of us enjoyed it."

Just then, the door opened and in walked Louise, Kurt, Stephanie, Renee and detective Stevens. They all gathered around Tracy's bed.

"We are all here for you Tracy. We know this is a very tough time for you right now, but you got my niece to think about. We all love and want what's best for you and that is to be here to raise our baby." Kurt said and the crowd said Amen even detective Stevens chimed in.

Tears began to roll down Tracy's face. She had never felt so loved by anyone other than Ron.

"I know you don't want to talk about this right now, but I made funeral arrangements for Ron. I want to have Ron and Trina's services together and buried together. I hope you understand."

"I know Martin told me and yes, I understand since she was a part of Ron's life for so long. I just wish this was all a dream."

"I know I do too."

"I have a big empty hole in my heart right now and it hurts like hell," Tracy said as the tear started coming again. Kurt moved closer and embraced her, careful not to touch her forehead.

"I know I feel the same damn way. I want this lady caught as soon as possible before I take matters into my own hands."

"If I wasn't pregnant, I would go and hunt that bitch on my own. And by the way, I am HIV negative."

"I am so glad to hear that," Louise said.

For the next several days, Tracy just went through the motions. She felt numb and unbalanced and if it wasn't for the people around her, she would probably try to commit suicide again. Life just didn't seem important to her right now without Ron. Ron was the first person besides Martin's fake ass that really cared about her. She thought, but what Tracy doesn't realize is that Martin truly loved her more than anything. He did his best to impress her and give her a nice life if only for a couple of months and when it boils down to it, Martin will be the one that will be there for her in the coming days when life is back to normal.

The day of the funeral Louise and Tracy walked around like zombies. Tracy had on one black and one blue shoe. No one noticed until they were at the funeral home. Shirley funeral home attendants did a great job. There were so many people in attendance for Ron and Trina. Trina looked so peaceful, but Ron had a scrawl on his face. I guess I would too if I left behind my unborn child that I wanted all my life, Tracy thought.

After the service, everyone made their way back to Ron's for dinner except for Trina's family. They didn't like the fact that Ron's girlfriend was living in Trina's and Ron's home. Tracy stayed upstairs in her room and ate her dinner with Martin. He refused to let her out of his sight. Renee was a little pissed about the attention Martin was giving Tracy and not her.

Renee couldn't take anymore and climbed the stairs to Tracy's room. Martin and Tracy were talking when they heard a knock at the door.

"Come in."

Renee opened the door and peeked in. "Martin, can I speak with to for a minute?"

"Sure," Martin said as he made his way to the door and stepped outside into the hall.

Renee closed the door behind him.

"I can't believe you. You're acting as if I'm not here."

"What are you talking about?"

"You haven't said two words to me today. You're so far up Tracy's ass you can't see anyone else."

"Renee she just lost her baby's father, she needs us right now. This is not the time to be selfish."

"So what we shared means nothing to you?"

"Pretty much."

"Fuck you, you asshole."

"I've been called worse," Martin said as he laughed watching Renee storm off.

Downstairs in the family room, Kurt, Stephanie, Detective Stevens and two of the officers were sitting watching television when Renee walked in. She didn't pay any attention to police hat that lay on the floor by the front door. She was so furious with Martin that she couldn't think straight.

"Where's Joe?" Larry asked.

"I don't know. I thought he went to the restroom." Detective Stevens said. "Well, it's about time for me to head home. I will check on you guys tomorrow." He said as he rose up off the couch and walked to the front door noticing the hat as well. Detective Stevens looked around to see if anything seemed out of the ordinary. Something told him something was up so instead of leaving, he pulled out his gun and slowly made his way upstairs to check on Tracy. Once he made it to her room, he tapped on the door lightly.

"Come in."

Detective Stevens opened the door slowly, entered the room and shut it behind him.

"I have a feeling something is not right." He whispered. Ed's hat is laying on the floor at the front door and he is nowhere in sight."

"Oh my God," Tracy said as she grabbed her chest.

"Don't worry Tracy you are safe. I'm going to text the officers downstairs to let them know my suspicions." Detective Stevens text both officers and waited for the responses. Five minutes went by and no response so he sends another text and waited and still no responses. Detective Stevens checks the room, the bathroom, the closet and outside on the balcony.

"You're safe here. Martin, I want you to stay here with Tracy locked the door when I leave and do not open this door until you hear my voice."

"Okay," Martin said.

Martin locked the door behind the detective and walked back to the bed with Tracy. They sat there in silence, wondering what the was going on.

Detective Stevens checked all the rooms upstairs before heading downstairs. He leaned over the balcony to see if he

209

saw anything before easing down the stairs. Just as he got to the bottom step, he heard a woman's voice, "Come on in here Detective Stevens and put your gun down and If you make one wrong move I will blow his head off."
Detective Stevens stood in the entryway of the family room. He saw a woman with a gun held up to Larry's head. "Lay your gun down and slowly kicked it to me."
Detective Stevens did as he was told to. Come in and have a seat on the couch. "Where's Martin and Tracy?"
No one said a word.

"Okay, I'm going to ask again, where's Tracy and Martin?"

"They flew out to LA right after the funeral services." Detective Stevens said.

"Do I look stupid to you? I know they're here in this house somewhere. I sat across from the house for hours and I saw them return with all of you. Now don't make me blow your fucking head off for lying to me. Now tell me where they are."

"Cynthia, why should I tell you anything? We all know you want them dead because you think they are carrying the HIV virus, but they're not. Martin tested negative and so did Tracy. Ron and Trina tested negative also. So it looks like you are the only carrier here."
Cynthia hit the detective in the back of the head with the butt of the gun. "How dare you lie to me like that? I know for a fact that Martin is HIV positive."

"No, you're the only one carrying that nasty disease." The detective said as he felt the back of his head and felt the blood gushing out.

"You killed people for no reason because you simply had your facts wrong," Kurt said in anger. "What did my brother do to you? You took him away from his unborn child. A child he wanted his entire adult life and because you're so fucking stupid, he's no longer here."

"Oh, so I'm stupid now?"

"You heard what I said," Kurt said.

"Oh, I will show you stupid," Cynthia said between coughs.

Cynthia walked over to Renee, pointed the gun to her forehead and pulled the trigger. "Now do I have to shoot all you motherfuckers because this is what stupid people do? Four down, two to go."

"If you think we're going to allow you to harm Tracy you are crazier than I thought," Kurt shouted trying to let Martin and Tracy hear him.

"What is going on?" Martin asked as he walked over to the door and quietly cracked the door open and just then, he recognized her voice.

CHAPTER TWENTY-THREE

Martin and Tracy moved to the balcony. This was their only way out. Martin jumped off the balcony with no problem. He steadied himself so he could catch Tracy without falling.

"Come on Tracy you can do it."

"Martin I'm scared."

"I know, but I will catch you, I promise. On the count of three, I need for you to jump."

"One, Two, Three." Tracy hollered as she jumped.

Downstairs in the family room, Cynthia stopped in her tracks. She was heading over to Kurt to punch the hell out of him when she heard a noise outside the home.

"What was that?" She asked as she walked over to the side of the window and looked out. She saw Martin and Tracy running across the yard to a neighbor's house and she took off out the door after them.

As the two ran, Tracy tripped and fall. Martin ran back to get her, but in doing so, Cynthia was right there. "Don't move or I will shoot her."

"Get your ass up," Cynthia said as she bent down and helped Tracy up by pulling on her arm.

"Martin get over here and stand by your bitch. I want you two to walk slowly toward the house and if either one of you makes one wrong move, I won't hesitate to shoot you both." Cynthia said as she pointed the gun.

Thank God for the nosy neighbors who saw the entire episode and called the police.

Back inside the house, Kurt, the officers, and detective Stevens came up with a plan. They waited inside the home for Cynthia to return. As she made her way inside the home and into the family room, Stephanie and Louise had run out the back while the men hid in their place.

Cynthia looked puzzled. Her plan had backfired and she was confused.

"Where the hell did everyone go?" Cynthia asked.

"What's wrong, things not going as planned," Tracy asked.

"Oh, they're going to go just as planned for your smart ass. Sit your ass down in that chair." It was the same chair that Renee was sitting in when she was shot.

"OMG!" Tracy yelled as she saw Renee's dead body on the side of the chair.

"Aw, don't worry, you will go quick and easy, just as she did."

"Like hell, I will," Tracy said as she ran toward Cynthia as fast as she could, and with her body, she rammed into Cynthia pushing her against the family room window and watched as Cynthia went through the glass.

When Cynthia looked up, she faced several cops with their guns drawn on her. She looked over at her gun that had fallen when she went through the window.

"Don't you dare think about it." One of the officers said. The officers grabbed Cynthia up off the ground, handcuffed her and escorted her to the police car.

"Keep still, you're only making it harder on yourself."

"Let me go you son of a bitch."

"Are you serious? With all the murders you committed you think I'm just going to let you go? What planet are you from?"

The officer helped Cynthia in the back seat of the car and shut the door.

"That was easy." He said, speaking to his fellow officers. Detective Stevens and the other officers came out. "I need some attention over here I was hit pretty hard in the back of my head." He said to one of the paramedics.

Louise and Stephanie stood on the back patio of one of the neighbors and figured it was safe to go over.

"Thanks so much for all of your help," Louise said to her neighbors.

"That's what neighbors are for."

Louise and Stephanie made their way around the front where all the commotion was. Stephanie spotted Kurt immediately and ran to him.

"Aw baby, I am so glad you're okay," Stephanie said as she wrapped her arms around her husband.

"Me too. This has been one hell of a day or should I say ordeal." They both laughed.

"I'm just glad it's over."

"I know. Are Martin and Tracy okay?" Stephanie asked.

"Yes, they are fine. Ms. Tracy pushed Cynthia through the family room window."

"What?"

"Yes, she's the hero. The paramedics are just checking her out right now."

"Can we go home? I am dying to sleep in my own bed."

"I know that feeling," Kurt said as they walked toward the paramedics to talk with Tracy before leaving.

The following week Kurt, Stephanie, Tracy, and Louise were at Jeff's the attorney. He had summoned them to come to hear the reading of Ron's will. Before Ron died, he changed his will to make sure that his daughter and Tracy would be well taken care of if anything should happen to him.

The family sat around the table and listened as Jeff spoke. "In Ron's will, he left his half of the business to his daughter and when she turns twenty- one, she could do as she pleases with her part of the business. He left his rental properties to Tracy Simmons, along with his present home, cars, bank accounts and finances. He left the house in Europe to his brother Kurt and the beach home in Hermosa to Tracy. Ron also made a stipulation that Louise would stay on with Tracy and if she decided not to, he left her a rental property to reside with an allowance of three thousand a month for the next ten years.

"If there are no questions, I think that about does it," Jeff said as he closed his briefcase.

The next several months Tracy's pregnancy was normal until her seventh month. She was confined to her bed. Martin helped Louise out with Tracy he was a godsend for Louise and Tracy. They don't know what they would have done if it wasn't for him, Kurt and Stephanie. They all took their turn in helping Louise out with Tracy.

"You guys have been so good to me and just know that I will make sure Ronisha knows how good you guys were. I know she will love you all just as much as I do." Tracy said with eyes filled with tears.

"Damn, if I get any bigger I will burst." Tracy joked with Kurt as he helped her out of bed so that Louise could change her bed sheets.

"I have no comment about that," Kurt said as he laughed.

"Stephanie and Kurt, if anything should happen to me, I want you guys to raise Ronisha, Okay."

"Are you serious?" Stephanie asked with joy in her heart.

"Yes, I wouldn't have it any other way."

"You got it," Kurt said as he smiled at his wife.
Martin walked in with desserts. "Look what I got?"

"Oh, you sure do know how to make a woman happy. Bring me that box over here right now."

"You do know you have to share with everyone," Martin said.

"So you think I'm going to eat all twelve doughnuts?" Martin shrugged his shoulders. "I know how much you like doughnuts, especially Longs."

Later that evening, Tracy and Louise was sitting downstairs at the kitchen table eating dinner when the doorbell rang.

"Let me guess, Martin. That man always comes at dinner time." Louise said as she got up from the kitchen table and answered the front door.

"Martin what a surprise, what are you doing in the neighborhood at dinner time?"

"Louise you know I cannot resist your cooking and besides you never invite me over for dinner so I have to keep inviting myself."

"You know you are more than welcome to have dinner with us on a regular basis," Louise said. She and Martin had become very close since the killings and him helping her out with Tracy. He was a part of the family now.

"Go on over there and fix your plate like usual."

"Everything smells so good."

"Louise, have you ever thought about opening your own restaurant?" Martin asked.

"Yes, I have thought about it many of times."

"So what happened?"

"At the time, I didn't have the money."

"Well, you have the money now. So what's stopping you?"

"You should do it," Tracy said.

"Well with the little one coming and all, I don't know."

"Louise I already told you I'm hiring a full-time nanny."

"In that case, I guess I could open my own restaurant, but I'm going to need help. I need to find the right location, hire the right staff and things like that."

"We can help you with that. You know Calvin is an awesome cook as well. He would love to work with you if you don't mind." Martin said.

The next few weeks, Tracy and Martin spent a lot of time together. She never asked Martin anymore about him and Ron, but it stayed on her mind. She could never see herself with a man who went both ways if that was the case with Martin so she kept her feelings for him strictly as a good friend or even a brother. Martin, on the other hand, wanted to take it slow with Tracy. He wanted to be more than just a friend, but he did not want to move too quick with her. He knew deep down inside that one day, he would have to explain the situation between Ron and himself. Martin knew that whatever he said could cause him to never be with the woman he truly loved so he was not looking forward to that and if it ever came to that, he would have to lie to keep from hurting her.

One night Tracy had just stepped out of the shower when her water broke.

"Oh my God! Martin, Louise someone help me!"

Tracy made her way over to the monitor and called for help again. Martin was there in no time.

"What's wrong Tracy?"

"My water just broke."

"Oh, the little one is coming," Louise said as she moved further inside the room. "Get her dress Martin while I get her overnight bag. I will call your doctor."

"Tracy your doctor wants to know how far your contractions are?"

"I'm not having any contractions."

"Okay, we will see you there. She wants us to take Tracy to the hospital, she said she will meet us there."

"Okay, mommy let's go," Martin said as he helped Tracy into the hall and down the stairs.

When Tracy made it to the hospital, she was still not having any contractions and had dilated to 5 centimeters. Her doctor decided to induce her contraction and after an hour later, she was able to inject the epidural.

"Oh, I feel so much better," Tracy said once the epidural kicked up.

"I hope you guys don't mind, but I'm taking a nap," Tracy said.

"Go right ahead, just as long as we can watch television, you can do whatever you want," Louise said as she stretched out on the couch while Martin sat in the chair.

Two hours later, Tracy awakens to pressure down in her vagina area. She called for the nurse and told her what she was feeling. The nurse examined Tracy again and by this time, she was ready to bring her baby girl into the world.

"Come on Tracy give me one more push." The doctor said.

One more push and Tracy brought into this world a 6-pound baby girl.

"Oh my God, there's one more." The doctor said.

"No, let her stay in there," Tracy said.

"Tracy sweetheart, you don't mean that," Martin said as he wiped Tracy's forehead with a cold cloth.

Tracy was amazed to see two little ones who looked exactly the same.

"You guys have to call Kurt and Stephanie. They are going to be so surprised just as I was." Tracy said.

Later that day, Kurt and Stephanie showed up with so many gifts for the twin girls. Kurt was disappointed that his brother wasn't there to see his beautiful girls. He knew he would be so thrilled and a very proud father. Kurt intended to let the girls know all about their dad. He wanted to keep Ron's spirit alive within his girls.

The next day, Tracy was released from the hospitals with her girls. Having two girls overwhelmed Tracy, but she was thankful for the nanny, she hired a week ago this took away a lot of stress for her she wondered if the nanny could handle both girls.

Louise, Martin, Kurt and Stephanie were so helpful. She didn't know what she would have done without them. Everyone spoiled the girls rotten. Ron would be so proud she thought as she stood over the girls as they slept. Ronisha and Ronita looked so much like Ron.

As the months went by, Martin had won Tracy's heart again. They talked about Martin's sexual escapade with Ron, which really wasn't anything sexual so he told her, but he knew if told Tracy the truth she would never allow him back into her heart. Martin hid the fact that Ron was jealous of how much attention Trina gave him and wanted to know why all the women were so crazy about the D so one night Ron and Martin were alone in the study having some drinks when Ron came on to him. He kissed Martin and Martin lead him into his room where they had sex and from that day forward, he craved Martin until Tracy came along. Martin and Ron would have sex every chance they got. Ron had given Martin the best oral sex he had ever had and that's what hooked him, but things came to a halt when Trina and Ron caught him in bed with their housekeeper. Trina went crazy and fired them both. She even fired Calvin because he knew all about this and never once informed her.

Four months later, Martin and Tracy flew to Hermosa Beach. Martin rented a yacht. The two ate, danced and made love all night. The next morning, Martin made breakfast and afterward, he proposed to Tracy. Tracy said yes, but she made one thing clear, she would never allow Martin to adopt the girls, she wanted the girls to always have Ron's last name until they married.

Martin and Tracy stayed on the yacht the entire week, but by this time, Tracy was eager to get home to her girls. Before they left, Louise made her promise not to call and check on the girls and so far, she kept that promise until today. She had never been away from them this long. She just wanted to call and let the girls hear her voice. Tracy dialed the number as Martin stood in front of her, shaking his head, but somehow he understood Tracy wanting to check on the girls. Tracy lets the phone ring for what seems like forever before hanging up.

"That's weird no one answered."

"Maybe they were busy or setting out back and didn't hear the phone," Martin said trying to ease Tracy's mind.

"Let me call Kurt and Stephanie just to see if they have been over since we left."

"Hey Stephanie, this is Tracy. How are you guys doing?" I was calling to see if you or Kurt had been to the house since we left? I called just a few minutes ago and I didn't get an answer?"

"Tracy I'm sure everything is fine. We stopped by the other day and all was well, but if it makes you feel any better Kurt and I will run over and check on the girls."

"Aw, I really would appreciate it, Stephanie."

"I will call you from the house."

"Okay and thanks again."
Later on that day, Kurt and Stephanie arrived and let
themselves in the house.

Tracy sat on the deck and enjoyed the warm air and the
sound of the waves beating up against the yacht.

"Honey, I'm not sure way Kurt and Stephanie have not
called us to let us know what's going on."

"I know it's not like them."
Martin could tell that Tracy was very uncomfortable, so he
called the house himself. When he didn't get an answer, he
called Kurt's cell phone and still no answer. Now he was
starting to worry.

"Why don't we just head home? We have enjoyed
ourselves tremendously so let's get back to our girls."

"I thought you would never say that," Tracy said as she
jumped up and hugged Martin.
Seven hours later, Martin and Tracy pulled into their
driveway and noticed Kurt and Stephanie's car.

"Um... that's strange." They didn't answer when I called
earlier and they never called us back to check in with us."
Martin said as he looked at Tracy strange.
As soon as Martin cut the engine, Tracy hopped out of the
car and ran up the walkway. She dug around in her purse for
her door key when she realized the door was opened. Tracy
pushed the door open, the smell almost knocked her down. It
smelled of something dead. Tracy froze in her tracks when
she saw Louise down the hall lying on the ground halfway
inside her room and out in the hallway.

"Oh my God! Martin." Tracy screamed. Martin was busy
getting their luggage when he heard Tracy. He dropped
everything and ran to her side. His mouth flew open as he
laid eyes on Louise.

"My babies Martin, my babies," Tracy whispered to
Martin too afraid to move and head up to the baby's room.
Martin was afraid of what he would find once he entered the
room. Martin grabbed a hold of Tracy's hand and pulled her

up the stairs with him. They both climbed the stairs slowly not sure what they would find once they were there. Martin and Tracy stood outside the girl's room. Martin looked back at Tracy before opening the door. The smell hit them before they even stepped foot inside the room. The smell told them what they needed to know. The smell of death was inside the room.

"Oh no! Not my babies." Tracy cried and screamed until she saw who she thought was the nanny, but it wasn't the nanny at all.

"What the hell happened here?" Tracy yelled out as she moved toward the intruder, but was stopped when the intruder raised her hand with a bloody knife in it. The nanny lunged at Tracy and stabbed her in the side. Martin tried to get to Tracy as soon as he could, but the movement in one of the baby's crib caught his attention and before he knew it, the nanny lunged at him. Martin fought the nanny off and someone how got a hold of the knife and stabbed the nanny until he tired.

The sound of Tracy moaning brought Martin back to reality. He moved to Tracy and held her. "Martin call 911 please."

The neighbors stood outside on their porch watching as the police and the coroner rushed inside the home. Lately, it had been one thing after another since Ron separated from Trina and moved in his girlfriend Tracy.

Cynthia sat down the street in her car as the tears fell from her eyes. She could not believe her sister was dead. She knew asking her sister to do this was putting her in danger, but her sister was always willing to do anything she asked. Now she regretted asking her, if only she had waited until she was out on bail to do the job herself her sister would still be alive.

"Martin brought all of this on himself. How could he have been so stupid not to see this coming? I tried to warn him on several occasions, but he continued to ignore me. He knew I was serious when I told him I would kill anyone he got involved with, but I guess I had to show him instead of telling him. Action always speaks louder than words." She said through her tear-filled eyes. Cynthia still loved Martin even after all the women he cheated on her with. He was her first love.

Cynthia consumed in her thoughts that she never saw the police officer approaching her car. The knock on the window startled her so she pulled off, leaving the officer standing.

On the way to the hospital with Tracy and the baby, Martin gets a call from Detective Stevens. "Martin I just found out that Cynthia has been released from jail. We will have guards posted outside of Ronisha's and Tracy's room at the hospital."

"What! Are you serious? How can someone who has murdered so many people be released from jail?"

"I can't say how, but it was a mix-up."
Martin tried to stay calm and not let Tracy worry about anything. He was concerned about her and Ronisha.

"I promise Martin I will not let anything happen to Tracy or Ronisha you have my promise. I'm heading to the hospital as we speak."
Martin sat down and laid his head against the wall of the ambulance. He looked over at Tracy, who had an oxygen mask on his heart ached for her. She had lost so much within the last five months that he didn't think she would pull out of it mentally. Then his mind went to Ronisha, he wondered what was going through her little mind as she was transported to the hospital.
Once they arrived at the hospital, Tracy was more concerned about Ronisha than for herself.

"Where's my baby?" Tracy cried out as the nurses rushed her back to the examining room.

"Martin, I want you to stay with Ronisha. Let her know that mommy's here." Tracy cried.

Three-month-old Ronisha was suffering from blunt force trauma to her head. She had bruises around her eyes and was covered in her sister's blood.

After Martin assured Tracy that Ronisha was going to pull through, she lay in bed thinking about everything that had happened to her this past year and realized she needed a clean start once she and baby Ronisha was released from the hospital.

This turned out to be one of the deadliest houses in Indianapolis. Six people were murdered here. Cynthia murdered one person and the intruder who turned out to be Cynthia's twin brother turned sister murdered the other five. Cynthia and her brother/sister Cindy had planned this when Cindy visited her sister in jail. The plan was to kill Tracy and Martin as well, but when they decided to go away, that changed things so Cindy went ahead with the plan and waited for Martin and Tracy to come back to kill them. Kurt and Stephanie weren't in the plan, but when they came by unexpectedly, Cindy had no choice but to kill them once Stephanie pushed her way inside the home followed closely by Kurt and saw Louise's dead body and tried to phone the cops.

Tracy's stab wound wasn't as bad as they thought, but once she was examined, they realized that she was three weeks pregnant. It turned out that Ronisha survived, but Ronita wasn't so lucky. She was now resting with her father, Louise, her aunt and uncle in heaven.

Ronisha wasn't out of the woods yet, but each day, she got better and better until Tracy was able to bring her home. Tracy and Martin no longer wanted the house on 9315 Primrose Street, it held too many bad memories. They knew it would be hard to sell, but they put it on the market anyway. They ended up selling all the rental property that

Tracy had inherited and decided to leave Indianapolis and to live in Los Angeles at their beach home in Hermosa Beach. Martin and Tracy married before leaving Indianapolis. They had a small ceremony at the justice of the peace and afterward, they boarded the plane to Los Angeles, leaving all the bad memories behind to get a new start on life for Ronisha and their unborn child, so they thought.

THE END

Well, I hope you enjoyed Scandalous. When I started writing this novel, I was headed in a different direction, but as you know, when you write, sometimes your characters take you in a totally different direction. I want to give my readers an opportunity to tell me how part 2 of this novel should go. You can email me at dhpublishingco@gmail.com or post your comment on my facebook page. Also, I have some questions below for those of you in a book club that may read this novel.

1. What did you think about the Martin character?
2. Was Tracy really a gold digger or did she simply want to live a good life?
3. What did you think about Trina and how she treated Ron?
4. Do you understand why Ron cheated with Tracy?
5. Was it right for Trina to leave her husband behind with their house guest?
6. Do you believe Renee and Gloria were really Trina's friends?
7. Have you ever encountered a person like Martin?
8. Would you be intrigued by a person like Martin?
9. Do most women want a man like Ron?
10. Do you know anyone who lives the life that Ron and Trina lived and do you think it would be worth it to have a man/husband that women hit on all the time because of what they could offer them?

ABOUT THE AUTHOR

Denise Hill was born and raised in Indianapolis, Indiana, where she resides today with her son Daniel and her daughter Devin. Today she works for herself at DH Publishing & Production Company, where she plans to turn her books into movies. Denise graduated from Thomas Carr Howe High School and received her Business degree from the University of Phoenix. Denise has always enjoyed writing and published her first novel in April 2014. This is her third novel and she is currently working on other novels and a movie.